"A strong drink will help. Then tell me all about it."

The Professor put out a firm but gentle hand. "I know the very place."

Rachel tried to pass him, but the professor was a bulky man. To her mortification her eyes filled with tears. "I don't want..." she began, but didn't go on.

The Professor's impersonal concern made him an easy man to talk to, and if she didn't talk to someone about the shock of seeing her own Melville with a very pretty girl, she would have hysterics.

Rachel got meekly into the Professor's Rolls-Royce when he held the door open, reflecting that it was nothing short of a miracle that he should appear just when she needed him—large, placid and extremely comforting.

Betty Neels is well-known for her romances set in the Netherlands, which is hardly surprising. She married a Dutchman and spent the first twelve years of their marriage living in Holland and working as a nurse. Today she and her husband make their home in a small ancient stone cottage in England's West Country, but they return to Holland often. She loves to explore tiny villages and tour privately owned homes there, in order to lend an air of authenticity to the background of her books.

Books by Betty Neels

HARLEQUIN ROMANCE

Off with the Old Love

Betty Neels

Harlequin Books

TORONTO • NEW YORK • LONDON
AMSTERDAM • PARIS • SYDNEY • HAMBURG
STOCKHOLM • ATHENS • TOKYO • MILAN

Original hardcover edition published in 1987
by Mills & Boon Limited

ISBN 0-373-02874-1

Harlequin Romance first edition November 1987

CHAPTER ONE

THE operation, a lengthy one, was, to all intents and purposes, over.

The man who had been bending over the still figure on the table for two hours or more straightened himself to his great height, spoke a few words to his registrar facing him, made sure that the anaesthetist was satisfied, peeled off his gloves and turned to his theatre sister.

'Thanks, Sister. I believe we caught him in time.' His voice was deep and quiet and rather slow and there were wrinkles at the corners of his eyes because he was smiling beneath his mask.

Rachel handed a needle holder to the registrar and a pair of scissors to the house surgeon assisting him. She said, 'Yes, sir, I'm glad,' and meant it. It had been a finicky case and she had watched Professor van Teule patiently cutting and snipping and plying his needle in his usual calm fashion. If he hadn't been successful she would have been genuinely upset; she had worked for him for two years now and they got on splendidly together. He was a first-rate surgeon, a brilliant teacher and a stickler for perfection, all of which he concealed under a laconic manner which new house surgeons sometimes mistook for too easy-going a nature, an error they quickly discovered for themselves. Rachel liked him and admired him; they had a pleasant relationship at work but where he lived or what kind of a life he led away from the operating theatre she had no idea, nor had she ever bothered to find out. His tall vast person, his handsome face and his pleasant voice were as familiar to her as the cloak she wrapped around herself going on and off duty: comfortable and nice to have around but taken for granted.

She nodded to one of the theatre nurses now and the girl slipped out of the theatre behind the Professor to take his gown and mask and warn Dolly, the theatre maid, that he would want his coffee, It was the last case on the morning's list and he had a teaching round at two o'clock. It was going on for one o'clock already and Rachel, with three brothers, had grown up with the conviction that a man needed to be fed regularly.

The registrar cast down his needle and put out a hand for the dressing and then stood back. 'You do it, Rachel. You're handy at it.'

He pulled off his gloves. 'That was a nice bit of needlework,' he commented. 'If ever I'm unlucky enough to be mown down by a corporation dustcart, I hope it'll be the Professor who is around to join the bits together again.'

'Refuse collector,' said Rachel, a stickler for the right word, 'and don't be morbid, George, you'll frighten Billy.'

She twinkled at the young house surgeon as she arranged the dressing just so and then stood away from the table while the patient was wheeled away to the recovery room.

'Coffee?' she asked, taking off her mask and gloves and standing still for one of the nurses to untie her gown. 'It'll be in the office . . . '

She went over to where her staff nurse was supervising the clearing away of the used instruments. She was a young woman, but older than herself, a widow with two children at school, and her firm friend.

'Norah, I'll be in the office. Professor van Teule wants his next list altered; I'll try and pin him down to doing it now before he disappears. Send Nurse Smithers to her dinner, will you? And Nurse Walters. Mr Sims's list isn't until two-thirty and we've got Mrs Pepys coming on at two o'clock.'

They exchanged speaking looks—Mrs Pepys, one of the part-time staff nurses, was tiresome and gave herself airs, talking down to the student nurses and reminding them all far too often that she was married to a descendant of the famous Samuel. 'We'll go to second dinner—at least, you go on time and ask them to keep mine for me, will you? And you scrub for the first case, I'll take the second and Mrs Pepys can take the third,'—Rachel's pretty face assumed a look of angelic innocence—'ingrowing toenails!'

A subdued bellow from the other end of the theatre corridor gave her no time to say more. She joined the Professor and his colleagues in her office and listened without rancour while the registrar and Dr Carr, the anaesthetist, made pointed remarks about women gossiping.

'Go on with you,' said Rachel mildly, on the best of terms with them both, and poured her coffee and then replenished the Professor's mug.

He was sitting on a quite inadequate chair which creaked alarmingly under his weight. 'That will give way one day,' she pointed out kindly. 'Won't you sit in mine, sir?'

'Only when you are not here, Rachel.' He watched her settle in her own chair. 'And now, this list of mine . . . '

They discussed the changes amicably. The Professor did not offer his reasons for starting his list at eight o'clock in the morning in three days' time, nor did Rachel evince the slightest curiosity as to why he expected her to struggle with her nurses' off duty rota and juggle it to suit. He took it for granted that she was prepared to be scrubbed and ready for him at an hour when she was usually in her office, coping with paperwork while her nurses got the theatre ready.

He got up to go presently, taking his registrar and the house surgeon with him. At the door he turned to ask casually, 'Your weekend off, Rachel?'

'Yes. The theatre's closed for cleaning, sir.'

He nodded. 'Well, enjoy yourself.'

He wandered off to cast a sharp eye over his patient in the recovery room and Rachel began to enter details of the day's work into her day book, dismissing him completely from her mind.

That done, she went along to theatre, to find Norah on the point of going to her dinner and the two junior nurses back on duty. She spent the next half-hour instructing them; they were very new to theatre work and a little scared and clumsy, but they were keen and they admired her hugely. A highly successful lesson was brought to its end by the appearance of Mrs Pepys, looking, as always, far too good for her surroundings. She bade Rachel good day and ignored the nurses.

'Hello,' said Rachel. 'We've laid up for the first case—staff's back in a few minutes, she'll scrub. You lay for the second case, please, and take the third . . . ' She paused on her way to the door. 'Ingrowing toenails.'

Mrs Pepys' exquisitely made-up face screwed itself into distaste. 'Sister, must I?'

Rachel's thick dark brows lifted. 'Staff's off duty early, I've a pile of book work, but if you don't feel you can cope . . . '

'Of course I can cope, Sister.' Mrs Pepys was furious at having her capabilities questioned but she didn't say so. Rachel was a calm, good-tempered girl, slow to anger and kind-hearted, but she was also a strict theatre sister and her tongue, once she was roused, had a nasty cutting edge to it.

With the two nurses safely in the anaesthetic room, making it ready, and Mrs Pepys huffily collecting instrument packs ready to lay up the second case, Rachel went off to her dinner.

There were only two other sisters still in the dining room: Lucy Wilson from the accident room, who, since accidents never occurred to fit in with the day's routine, was seldom at meals when everyone else was, and Sister Chalk, verging on retirement but still bearing the reputation of being a peppery tyrant. Rachel, who had trained under her on Men's Medical, still treated her with caution.

Conversation, such as it was, was confined largely to Sister Chalk's pithy opinion of the modern nurse, with Lucy and Rachel murmuring from time to time while they gobbled fish pie—always fish on Fridays—and something called a semolina shape. Presently they excused themselves and went their different ways. Dolly would have put a tray of tea in the office and Rachel, with five minutes to spare, was intent on reaching it as quickly as possible.

She took the short cut along the semi-basement passage, thus avoiding the visitors who would be pouring into the entrance hall and the wards, then took the stairs at the end two at a time to teeter on the top tread as Professor van Teule, appearing from the ground under her feet, put out a large arm to steady her.

'Oh, hello, sir,' said Rachel and beamed at him. He towered over her, but, since she was a big girl herself and tall, she had never let his size worry her. 'Short cut, you know.'

'I often use it myself,' he told her placidly and let her go. He stood aside so that she could pass him and with another smile and a nod she started off along the passage which would bring her out in the theatre wing. He stood and watched her go, his face impassive, before he trod down the stairs.

Rachel hadn't given him a second thought; she had five minutes more of her dinner time still. She hurried into her office, saw with satisfaction that the tea tray was on her desk, and stationed herself before the small square of mirror on the wall, the better to powder her nose and tidy her hair beneath her frilled cap. Her reflection was charming: big dark eyes, a straight nose—a little too long for beauty—and a generous mouth, the whole framed in glossy dark brown hair, wound into a thick plaited bun. She pulled a face at herself, rammed a hairpin firmly into place and sailed into the corridor on her way to theatre, where Norah was dealing competently with Mrs Pepys's airs and graces and the junior nurses' efforts to be helpful. There was a good ten minutes in hand. The two staff nurses joined her for tea and then went back to theatre so that the two student nurses might have theirs.

Rachel settled down to her desk work, interrupted almost at once by the arrival of Mr Sims and the anaesthetist who, of course, wanted tea as well. They were joined presently by Billy, who, since there was no more tea in the pot, contented himself with the biscuits left in the tin.

'What is the first case, Rachel?' asked Mr Sims, who knew quite well.

'That PP—left inguinal hernia. Norah's scrubbing.'

'I want you scrubbed for the second case.'

'Yes, I know, sir,' said Rachel tranquilly. 'It's that nasty perf.'

'And the last?' Mr Sims was a shade pompous but he always was.

'Ingrowing toenail. Mrs Pepys will scrub.' She added, 'Is Billy doing it?'

'Good idea. That will allow me to leave George to keep an eye on him.'

The afternoon went well with none of the hold-ups which so often lengthened a list. Norah went off duty at four o'clock, and the heavy second case was dealt with by five o'clock, leaving Billy to tackle the ingrowing toenail. By six o'clock everyone but Rachel and one nurse had gone and, leaving her colleague to finish cleaning the theatre and readying it for the night, Rachel sat down once more to finish her books. She would be off duty at eight o'clock and had every intention of driving home that evening. She allowed her thoughts to stray to the two days ahead of her and sighed with anticipatory pleasure before finishing her neat entries.

She had a bed-sitting room in the nurses' home because, although she would have preferred to live out, there was always the chance that she might be needed on duty unexpectedly. She sped there as soon as she had handed over the keys to the night staff nurse, and tore into the clothes she had put ready—a tweed skirt and a sweater, for the evenings were still chilly at the

end of March—snatched up a jacket and her overnight bag, and, pausing only long enough to exchange
a word here and there with such of her friends as were
off duty, hurried down to the car park where her car,
an elderly small Fiat, stood in company with the
souped-up vehicles favoured by the younger housemen
and divided by a thin railing from the consultants'
BMWs, Mercedes and Bentleys. As she got into the
Fiat she glanced across to their stately ranks; Professor
van Teule's Rolls Royce wasn't there. Fleetingly, she
wondered where it was and then dismissed the thought
as she concentrated on getting out of London and on
to the M3 as quickly as possible.

Her home was in Hampshire, some fifty miles
distant—a pleasant old house on the edge of the village
of Wherwell, with a deep thatched roof and a garden
full of old-fashioned flowers in which her mother
delighted. She had never lived anywhere else; her father
had been the doctor there for thirty years and, since
her eldest brother intended to join him in the practice,
she supposed that it would always be home.

The streets were fairly empty and Rachel made good
time. Once on the M3, she pushed the little car to its
limit until she came to the end of the motorway and
took the Andover road, to turn off at the crossroads
by Harewood Forest. She was almost home now. She
drove through the quiet village and presently saw the
lights of her home.

She turned in at the open gateway and stopped at
the side of the house. Her father had the kitchen door
open before she had got out of the car and she went
joyfully into the warmth of the room beyond. Her
mother was there and her eldest brother, Tom.

'Darling! So nice to see you.' Her mother gave her a great hug. 'You'll want your supper . . . '

Her father kissed her cheek. 'Had a good trip from the hospital?' he wanted to know. 'You look very well.'

Tom gave her a brotherly slap. 'Revoltingly healthy,' he pronounced, 'and putting on weight, too.'

'No—am I? There's too much of me already.' She grinned cheerfully at his teasing. 'How are Edward and Nick?'

'Doing well.' It was her father who answered. 'Edward's done excellently in his exams and Nick's settling down nicely.'

They had sat down at the old-fashioned table with its Windsor chairs at each end and the smaller wheel-backs, three each side. They were joined by Mutt, the labrador, and Everett, the family cat, who sat quietly while they had the soup and cold ham, taking a long time over them for there was so much to talk about.

'How's Natalie?' Rachel wanted to know, passing her cup for more tea.

'Fine. She's coming over tomorrow.' Tom had got engaged to a girl in the next village—the vet's daughter and someone they had all known for most of their lives. 'How about your Melville?'

Melville was a producer in television and it was because of him that Rachel neither noticed nor encouraged the advances of quite a few of the medical staff at the hospital. She was quite prepared to be friendly but that was all; she was wholly loyal to Melville and, being a modest girl, had never quite got over her delight and surprise when he had made it clear, after they had met at a party, that he considered her to be his. True, he hadn't mentioned getting married, but he took her out and about, sent her flowers and , when she had firmly refused to spend a weekend at Brighton with him, had taken her refusal with good grace and no hard feelings. Indeed, he had somehow made her feel rather silly about it and she was honest enough to agree with him. She was, after all, twenty-five and sensible. Too sensible, perhaps. She smiled. 'Up to his eyes in work but he's collecting me for a drink on Sunday evening. I've got to be back because Professor van Teule wants to operate at eight o'clock on Monday morning.'

Her father lifted an eyebrow. 'Working you hard? Something tricky?'

'No, the usual list—most of his cases are tricky, anyway. I expect he wants to get away early.'

'You like working for him still, darling?' asked her mother.

'Oh, yes. He's always good-natured and easy—we get on famously.'

Her mother gave an inward regretful sigh. She had met Melville only once, and she hadn't taken to him. This Professor sounded nice—he would be married, of course, and probably middle-aged . . . She asked, 'How old is he?'

Rachel bit into an apple. 'Do you know, I've no idea? Anything between thirty-five and forty-five, I suppose. I've never looked to see.'

They cleared the supper dishes and then, since it was now late, went to bed.

The weekend went too quickly. Rachel, country born and bred, wondered for the hundredth time what on earth had possessed her to choose a job which forced her to live in London. But she had never wanted to do anything else and her family had let her go at eighteen to train at one of the big London teaching hospitals and made a great success of it, too. They were proud of her, although her mother's pride was thinned by the wish that Rachel would marry, but she never mentioned this.

Rachel drove back after tea; Melville wouldn't be free until half-past eight and she had plenty of time. It was a blustery evening and there was little traffic, even on the motorway. She parked the Fiat and made her way to her room where she changed into a dark brown suit and a crêpe blouse and exchanged her sensible low-heeled shoes for high heels. Melville liked well-dressed women; indeed, he didn't care for her job since, as he explained to her in his well modulated voice, it necessitated her wearing the most outlandish clothes.

'Well, I'd look a fool tripping round the theatre in high heels and a smart hat,' Rachel had pointed out reasonably, not really believing him.

She had ten minutes to spare; she nipped along to the little pantry the sisters shared in their corridor and found Lucy making tea. Melville had said drinks, which probably meant nothing but bits and pieces to eat with them and she had had no supper. 'Mother gave me a fruit cake,' she said. 'Bring that pot of tea with you and have a slice.'

Lucy followed her back to her room and kicked the door shut. 'Going out? It's a beastly night but I suppose Melville will see you don't get cold and wet. I like the shoes—new, aren't they?'

Rachel agreed guiltily. Since she had started going out with Melville she had spent more on clothes than she could afford, and they were the kind of clothes she wouldn't normally have bought. Her taste ran to tweed suits and simply cut jersey dresses with an occasional splurge on something glamorous for the hospital ball or some special occasion.

She drank her tea and gobbled up her cake. 'I must fly . . . ' She took a last look in the mirror and Lucy said laughingly, 'Do him good to be kept waiting, and you needn't bother to prink; you look good in an old sack.'

Rachel gave her jacket a tug. 'I'm getting fat,' she worried. 'It doesn't notice because I'm tall, but it will—Melville doesn't like fat girls.'

'You're not fat.' Lucy picked up the teapot, preparatory to departing to her own room. 'Just generously curved. There is a difference. Have fun, love.'

Melville's car wasn't in the forecourt. Rachel peered round hoping to see him and then took a backward step back into the entrance hall. Her heel landed on something yielding and she turned sharply to find herself face to face with Professor van Teule's solid front.

She said guiltily, 'I'm so sorry—have I hurt you badly? I had no idea . . . '

He glanced down at his elegantly shod foot. 'I scarcely noticed.' He eyed her deliberately. 'You're very smart. Going out for the evening? If he's not here you'd better come inside—you'll catch a cold standing here.'

She obeyed his matter-of-fact advice, and, when he enquired if she had had a pleasant weekend, said that yes, she had. 'But over too soon—it always is.' She glanced at his placid face. 'Is there a case in theatre? You're here . . . '

'There was. I'm on my way home.'

She hardly heard him. Melville's Porsche had stopped outside and he was opening the entrance door and coming towards them. She half glanced at the

Professor, a polite oodbye on her tongue, only he wasn't going away; he stood, completely at ease, watching Melville who caught her hand and cried, 'Darling, I'm late. Do forgive me—I got caught up at the studio. You know how it is.'

She said hello and added almost crossly, 'This is Professor van Teule—I work for him. Professor, this is Melville Grant—he's in television.'

'How very interesting,' observed the Professor. 'How do you do, Mr Grant.' He didn't shake hands, only smiled in a sleepy way and patted Rachel on a shoulder. 'Don't let me keep you from your free evening.'

He went on standing there, so that after a minute Rachel murmured a goodbye and went to the door with Melville at her heels.

It shouldn't have been like that, she thought peevishly—he should have walked away instead of seeing them off the premises like a benevolent uncle.

Melville opened the car door for her with something of a flourish. He gave a quick glance behind him as he did so to see if the Professor was watching. He was.

'Sleepy kind of chap, Professor What's-his-name. Don't know that I'd care to have him nod off over my appendix or whatever.'

Womanlike, Rachel sprang at once to the defence of the man who had annoyed her. 'You couldn't have a better surgeon,' she declared roundly, 'and he's far too busy to do appendicectomies—he specialises in complicated abdominal surgery and he's marvellous with severe internal injuries; even when it seems hopeless, he . . . '

Melville drove out of the forecourt. 'My dear girl, spare me the gruesome details, I beg you. Tell me, did you have a happy time with your family? I can see that it did you good, you're more beautiful than ever.'

Something any girl would like to hear and, to a girl in love, doubly welcome. 'Lovely, but far too short.'

He had turned the car in the direction of the West End. 'I thought we might have a drink . . . ' He named a fashionable club. 'I had dinner with the producer and you will have had a meal, of course.'

Rachel had her mouth open to say that she hadn't but she had no chance to speak, for he went on, 'There's a party next week—you simply must come, darling. Buy yourself something eye-catching; everyone who's anyone will be there.'

She thought guiltily of the dresses she had bought in the last few months, worn a few times and then pushed to the back of the wardrobe because Melville had hinted, oh, so nicely, that to be seen more than a couple of times in the same dress just wasn't on. She said quietly, 'I'll have no chance to go shopping and I'll be too whacked to go to any parties.' She turned to smile at him. 'You'll have to find another girl, Melville.'

She had meant it as a joke; his easy, 'It looks as though I'll have to,' took her by uneasy surprise. She spent the next minute or two mentally reviewing the next week's lists and the off-duty rota. It was take-in week, too; there was no way in which she could alter the unalterable schedule.

'Well, let's worry about it later,' said Melville and parked the car.

The club was brightly lit and very full. It was also elegantly furnished. They were ushered to a table a little to one side and Melville at once began to point out the well-known people around them. When a waiter came he turned to Rachel. 'You need bucking up, darling. How about vodka?'

She could hardly mention her empty stomach. Instead she murmured that it gave her a headache and could she have a long cold drink?

Melville shrugged in tolerant good humour. 'Of course, my sweet. What shall it be?'

'Tonic with lemon and ice, please.' She sat back and looked around her. The suit she was wearing had no chance against the ultra-chic women there, but that didn't worry her overmuch, just as long as Melville liked what she wore.

Their drinks came and with them a dish of *crudités*, some salted nuts and potato straws. None of them filling, but better than nothing. She nibbled a few carrot sticks and crunched a potato straw while Melville turned his head to wave to an acquaintance. He turned back presently and began on a long and amusing story about the production he was working on. He was handsome and entertaining and paid her extravagant compliments which she never quite believed. Not that that mattered, for he was in love with her; he had told her so many times. One day he would ask her to marry him and she was sure she would say yes. Her eyes shone at the thought so that Melville paused in what he was saying; she really was a remarkably pretty girl, although she was proving disappointingly stubborn about taking more time off. 'Let's go somewhere and dance?' he suggested.

She said with real regret, 'Oh, Melville, I can't. We start work at eight o'clock tomorrow morning and I'll have to be on duty before then.'

He frowned and then laughed and caught her hand. 'You really are the most ridiculous girl I've ever met.

I could get you a part in my next production, or find you some modelling work, but you choose to spend your days in your revolting operating theatre.'

'I don't want to do anything else. It's not revolting, either.'

He picked up her hand and kissed it. 'You dear creature, so earnest. Tell you what, I'll pick you up tomorrow evening when you're off duty and we'll go somewhere and have a meal.'

'It's take-in week. I might get held up, but I'd love that. Somewhere where I won't need to dress up, Melville.'

'The nearest Lyons,' he assured her laughingly. 'And now, before you say it, you want to get back, don't you? Duty calls and so on.'

They took some time to get out of the club; Melville stopped so many times to greet people he knew. Rachel felt very proud of him. Sometimes, but not always, he introduced her with a casual, 'Meet Rachel,' and she smiled at faces which showed no interest in her and listened politely to what they had to say, although none of it made much sense to her.

At the hospital he leaned over and opened her door and then kissed her. 'I won't get out, darling,' he told her. 'I must go back to the office and work for a while.'

She was instantly worried. 'Oh, not because you took me out?' she wanted to know. 'Now you'll have to stay up late working . . . '

'I'd stay up all night for you, darling.' He smiled as he closed the door and with a wave shot away.

Rachel went to her room, made a pot of tea, ate the rest of the cake and put her uniform ready for the morning. Lying in a hot bath she mulled over her evening; it had been delightful, of course, because

Melville had been with her, but hunger had taken the gilt off the gingerbread. It was a pity, she mused, that she was in love with a man who didn't always remember to ask her if she were hungry, while there were several young men on the medical staff who would have whisked her off to the nearest café for a meal at her merest hint . . . She frowned. It was strange that, whereas she would have no hesitation in telling any one of them that she was hungry, she found herself unable to tell Melville.

She got into bed, meaning to lie and think about him. He was very good-looking, she reflected sleepily, not tall but always so beautifully turned out. He wore his dark hair rather long and his voice was soft and his speech clipped. On the edge of sleep, she found herself comparing it with Professor van Teule's deep slow tones—not a bit alike, the two of them; the professor was twice the size for a start . . .

The Professor walked into the theatre at exactly eight o'clock and Rachel, however easygoing his manner was, had taken care to have everything ready. Sidney, the theatre technician, was standing ready, her nurses were positioned where they would be most required, Dr Carr and his patient were there, the latter already nicely under, and she herself stood, relaxed with her trolleys around her. He bade everyone good morning and she watched his casual glance taking everything in; he expected perfection and she took care that he got it. George and Billy had taken up their places and the Professor waited quietly while they arranged sterile sheets round the patient before putting out a hand for a scalpel.

It would be a lengthy operation—a gastroduoden-ostomy—but since most of the Professor's work was major surgery, involving all the clap-trap modern methods could devise, Rachel went placidly ahead with what was required of her, by no means disturbed by the paraphernalia around her. She sent the nurses in turn to their coffee, and then Norah, and when at last the Professor stood back from the table, she nodded to the nurse nearest the door to warn Dolly that coffee would be a welcome break.

The patient borne carefully away, the other men followed the Professor and Rachel stripped off her gown and gloves, made sure that Norah was laying up for the next case, and went along to her office. There was no room for them all, but somehow they fitted themselves in and left her chair empty. She poured the coffee and handed round the biscuit tin and, since the Professor had already had his, handed him the patient's notes when he asked for them. He sat hunched up on the radiator, writing up the details of the operation, while the others discussed where they hoped to go for their holidays.

'What about you, Rachel?' asked Dr Carr.

George grinned across at her. 'Oh, our Rachel will be on her honeymoon—somewhere exotic.'

She coloured at that although she answered matter-of-factly, 'Chance is a fine thing—I can't very well have a honeymoon without a husband.'

She was aware that the Professor had stopped writing and was looking at her but she didn't look at him. Although she had to when he asked casually, 'Did you have a pleasant evening, Rachel?'

The look was grateful; it gave the conversation a turn

in a different direction. She didn't mind being teased in the least—three brothers had inured her to that— but somehow she was shy of talking about Melville.

'Lovely,' she told him. 'We went to a club—I've forgotten its name—and it was full of beautiful models and the kind of people you see on the TV.' She put down her mug. 'I'll see if they are ready for you, sir.'

He glanced at his watch. 'We're behind time. George, I may have to leave the last case to you, but I'll be in this evening.' He got to his feet and went unhurriedly to scrub.

The morning wore on. The nurses went in turn to their dinners and two of them went off duty. Norah, back from her own dinner, was laying up in the second theatre for the afternoon list, a short one—dentals— which she would take and then go off duty for the evening. Rachel had intended taking an afternoon off, but as the hands of the clock crept towards two, she resigned herself to much less than that. The Professor had changed his mind and decided to do that last case himself—a good thing as it turned out for it presented complications which he hadn't expected. When at last the patient had been wheeled away it was half-past two.

'Sorry about this, Rachel,' he said. 'You've missed your dinner. Do you suppose they would send up sandwiches for us both? I've an appointment in less than an hour and so can't spare the time for a meal.'

George and Billy had already left. Rachel left two student nurses to start clearing up, went to have a word with Norah, waiting for her first patient, then went along to phone the canteen. She found the Professor putting down the receiver. 'I thought they might be a good deal quicker if I rang—you don't mind?'

She was pinning her cap on to her wealth of hair. 'Not a bit—they'll fall over themselves to get here. Dolly's making coffee.'

Five minutes later they were sitting opposite each other at the desk eating roast beef sandwiches with the added niceties of horseradish sauce and pickles, some wedges of cheese and, for the Professor, a bottle of beer.

'Well,' said Rachel, happily sinking her teeth into the beef, 'is this what you get when you ask for sandwiches? I get two cheese left over from the day before and a nasty snort down the phone as well.'

'That won't do at all. You're no sylph-like girl to exist on snacks; I'll look into it. Did you have a splendid supper last night?'

His voice was quiet but he glanced at her with intentness. There was something about his calm placidity which invited confidences

'*Crudités.* Melville thought I'd had supper and he'd had dinner anyway.'

'My dear girl, surely you could have hinted . . . '

She considered this. 'Not really. It was so—so . . . ' She was at a loss for a word.

He said smoothly, 'The surroundings were not conducive to a plate of steak and kidney pudding?'

'That's exactly it. Anyway, I eat too much.'

His inspection of her person was frank and impersonal. 'You're a big girl and you use up a lot of energy; it would be hard for you to eat too much.'

'Oh, good,' said Rachel and took another sandwich.

The Professor passed her the pickles. 'You're on until eight o'clock? Let us pray for no emergencies.'

Perhaps he didn't pray hard enough. Just as Rachel was closing the last of her books preparatory to sending the junior nurse off duty before going herself, the phone rang.

It was Lucy. 'Rachel, there's a gunshot wound coming in and coming up to you as soon as we can manage it. Abdominal and chest. George is here now and intends to ring Professor van Teule. Have you got a nurse on?'

'Little Saunders; Sidney Carter's on call, I'll give him a ring.' It sounded like a case where the theatre technician might be needed.

She went about the task of getting the theatre ready with Nurse Saunders, keen as mustard but easily put off by anything she didn't quite understand, trotting obediently to and fro.

Rachel was checking the special instruments that might be needed when the phone went again. The Professor, coming through the theatre corridor doors, answered it. A moment later, he put his head round the theatre door.

'For you, Rachel. Melville, I believe.'

'Oh, I can't . . . ' she began, and then said, 'I'd better, I suppose.'

Melville was downstairs, phoning from the porter's lodge, something strictly not allowed. 'Put on your prettiest dress, darling,' he begged her, 'we're going to a party. I'll give you fifteen minutes.'

'Melville, I can't possibly. I'm on duty and there's an emergency case coming up any minute.'

'Well, hand over your revolting tools to someone else, dear girl. This is some party.'

She said tartly, 'You'll have to find somebody else, Melville. I'm on duty.'

'It's gone eight o'clock. You told me that you were off duty then.'

'Well, I am usually, but not when there's an emergency.'

His voice sounded cold and faintly sneering. 'Darling, aren't you just the weeniest bit too good to be true?'

He hung up, leaving her shaking with unhappy rage, and the Professor, who had been standing in the doorway, unashamedly listening, took the receiver from her and replaced it.

'Is there anyone we can get to take over from you?' he asked and his voice was very kind. 'Night sister? Norah?'

She gave him an indignant look. 'Certainly not, Professor. I'm on duty, and in any case I'm not in the mood for parties.' She added unhappily, 'I've nothing to wear—I mean, he has seen the dresses I've got at least six times.'

'That is a point,' agreed the Professor gravely. 'I have no doubt that, to a man in his type of job, clothes matter a great deal.'

Rachel nodded. 'Oh, they do, and you see I've never bothered a great deal—I mean, not to fuss, if you know what I mean? Brothers never notice what you're wearing anyway . . . ' She stopped suddenly. 'I'm sorry—talking to you like this; I quite forgot who you were.'

If the Professor found this remark a little surprising, he gave no sign. He said soothingly, 'I am sure you will have an opportunity to go out with, er, Melville again.' He became businesslike. 'This man who is coming up—gunshot wounds at close range—I've had a look and we'll need a lot of luck on our side. How are you off for staff?'

She cast him a grateful look. He never failed to see that she had enough help. 'If Billy is here, I can manage. I've a junior on—very new but eager—and Carter's coming in.'

'He's a good man to have about. Right, I'll take a look at what you've put out, shall I?'

They went over the instruments together and then he went away, leaving her to scrub and get into her gown and mask and gloves and lay up.

Dr Carr would be anaesthetising; she had expected that. The Professor and he had worked together for a year or two now. He appeared with his patient and a nurse from the accident room to attend to his wants and keep an eye on the drip they had set up. The Professor, with George and Billy, followed hard on his heels.

It took a very long time; it was an hour short of midnight when at last the Professor finished his patchwork, meticulously done with tiny stitches and infinite patience. He thanked them all, as he always did, and left George to do the tidying up before the man was taken to the intensive care unit.

Rachel started to clear up, and Nurse Saunders, still game, toiled with her until two night nurses appeared to help. Things went more quickly then and presently Rachel and Nurse Saunders were able to take off their gowns and masks and go off duty. But not yet, it seemed. As they went down the corridor George came to meet them. 'There's food and drink in the office—we're all having a picnic; come on.'

The Professor had been exerting his charm again. There were sandwiches and a dish of sausages, a bowl of crisps and a great jug of coffee.

'However did you get this lot?' asked Rachel and sat Nurse Saunders down in front of the sausages.

'It's a kind of blackmail,' he explained gravely. 'You see, if the kitchen superintendent keeps me well fed, she feels pretty sure that, should she need my help at any time, I shall give it gladly and with expertise.'

Rachel forgot the time, that she was tired, that she had missed a glamorous evening with Melville. She looked round at her companions, very contentedly munching, and thought of the man they had worked so hard to save. She would have missed a dozen evenings out just for the satisfaction of knowing that the patient would recover, and as for her companions, she couldn't think of any better. She caught the Professor's eye and he smiled at her.

'Not very elegant and none of us look fashionable, but there's a satisfaction . . . '

She beamed at him, her mouth full. He was right, but then he always was.

CHAPTER TWO

PERHAPS it was a good thing that there was a sudden spate of emergencies; Rachel had very little time to wonder why Melville didn't phone her, although the nagging thought that he was angry with her was at the back of her mind. She could, of course, phone him, but even after the four days of silence from him she couldn't bring herself to do that. She loved him, she had no need to tell herself that, but she also held a responsible job and he would have to try to understand that.

It was on the fifth evening, after a gruelling day, that she found him in the entrance hall as she was going off duty. Her tired face lit up at the sight of him although her, 'Hello, Melville,' was uttered in a matter-of-fact voice.

Melville wasn't in the least matter-of-fact. He swooped upon her, his handsome face all smiles. 'Darling, you're off duty? Nip along and put on something pretty—I've got a table at the Savoy and we'll find somewhere to dance.'

She said uncertainly, 'I'm tired, Melville; it's been a busy day. If we could go somewhere quiet . . . '

'Nonsense, darling, what you need is some fun and a drink or two. I'll give you fifteen minutes.'

She thought longingly of supper, a hot bath and blissful bed, but what were they compared to Melville? She said quietly, 'All right, fifteen minutes.'

She showered and changed into what she hoped would pass muster at the Savoy and, because she had cut it rather fine, took the short cut past the consultants' room. There would be no one about as late as this, she told herself, but skidded to a halt as the door opened and the Professor came out.

His look of astonishment left her without words. 'My dear, girl,' he said. 'You're going out on the town?' His lazy gaze swept over her nicely made-up face and the blue dress she hoped would meet the occasion. 'You were rocking on your feet,' he observed. 'It should have been supper, bath and bed.' He added. 'I've that nephrectomy first thing tomorrow—you'll need to be on your toes.'

Rachel stared up at his placid face. 'He's here— Melville. I've not heard from him all week, ever since . . . He wants to take me out to dinner and then go dancing.' She hesitated. 'You see, Professor, I can't not go—so often he asks me out and I'm not free, and I'm so afraid he'll . . . '

A large comforting hand came down on her shoulder. 'Of course—a dry old stick such as myself tends to overlook the first fine raptures of first love. Why not give yourself a morning off? Norah can scrub.'

She said indignantly, 'Certainly not, Professor,' and went on ruefully, 'I'm sorry, I didn't mean to say it like that. It's kind of you to suggest it, but I shall be all right.'

'Good. Run along then, and enjoy yourself.'

She wished him goodnight and almost ran the rest of the way, wondering why on earth she should imagine that behind that placid face he was amused about something.

Melville was impatient although he hid it very successfully. 'They'll keep our table', he assured her as he hurried her out to the car. 'You're wearing that blue dress again—a mistake, darling, you haven't enough colour for it.'

Rachel, indignation for once swamping her love, snapped, 'I've been hard at work all day and I'm tired—I did tell you . . . '

He had got into the car beside her and now he leaned over and kissed her. 'My poor darling, you'll feel fine after a meal.'

She did her best; the food was delicious andMelville at his most amusing, but her heart wasn't in it. When they had had their coffee she said contritely, 'Melville, do you mind very much if we don't go dancing? I really am tired.'

She was happily surprised when he leaned across the table and took her hand in his. 'My poor sweet, I'll take you straight back. Get to bed and have a good sleep— get someone to bring you your breakfast . . . '

There wasn't much point in telling him that she would be getting up at seven o'clock, and as for being brought breakfast in bed . . . There was, she realised, a wide gap between his world and hers, but that gap would disappear in time. She gave him a grateful smile. 'I've spoilt your evening and I'm sorry—I'll do better next time.'

He pressed her hand and smiled at her. A charming smile which made her happy, as it was meant to. She felt happy still as he drove her back to the hospital, kissed her goodnight, and then drove away at once. She opened the door and wandered through the entrance hall on her way to the back corridor leading to the nurses' home. She had almost reached it when she

became aware that Professor van Teule was watching
her from the massive staircase at the back of the hall.

She crossed the hall and met him at the bottom step.
'Has there been something in theatre?' she wanted to
know urgently, quite forgetting the 'sir'.

He smiled and shook his head. 'I came to check on
that transplant we did this morning.' He stood there
quietly, waiting for her to speak.

'I've had a simply lovely evening,' she said at last,
defiantly, just as though she expected him to contra-
dict her, unaware that her pretty face was white and
pinched with fatigue. And, when he nodded gently,
'Goodnight, Professor.'

'Goodnight, Rachel.' He watched her go back down
the passage and through the door at its end before he
crossed the entrance hall and got into his car.

Rachel slept like a log and only her long training in
early rising got her out of bed in the morning. She went
down to a breakfast she didn't want, immaculate as
always but her face pale and shadows under her eyes.
She gulped tea, crumbled toast and then went on duty.
Norah was laying up for the nephrectomy and the
student nurses were trotting to and fro. Rachel bade
them good morning, cast an eye over what was being
done and went to her office. The usual small pile of
paperwork was on her desk. She pushed it aside,
checked with the accident room that there was nothing
in the way of an emergency, then went through to the
anaesthetic room to do a final check. Dr Carr was
already there, adjusting his machines; he glanced up as
she went in and then gave her asecond longer look.

'Rachel, my dear girl, you look like skimmed milk.
Haven't you slept?'

She managed a bright smile. 'I slept like a top, whatever that means. I'm fine.' She glanced at the clock. 'Shall I phone the ward to send up the patient?'

He nodded. 'If you're ready. Professor van Teule will be here in in about five minutes.'

She swept away and did that and then started to scrub. She was gowned and gloved when the patient was wheeled in with Dr Carr at his head. A moment later the Professor, with George and Billy beside him, started to scrub. She was on the point of taking up her usual place behind her trolleys and replied composedly to their good mornings and stood just as calmly waiting for them to come into the theatre. She didn't feel calm; she had a nasty headache and it was too late now to take anything for it.

The nephrectomy wasn't straightforward; the Professor seemed to attract complicated cases like honey attracts bees; moreover, he didn't seem to mind. Other surgeons in like circumstances would give vent to strong language, not caring who heard them, but he, beyond muttering in his own tongue, which nobody there understood anyway, remained as placid as usual.

He was putting the final touches to his work when he addressed Rachel.

'I should like to do a transplant—kidney—on a young man. Could you arrange things so that you will be available—and such of your nurses as you will need?' He glanced at her. 'It will probably be during the night or the very early morning but I am told that the donor is in a coma and not likely to live for very long.'

'I'll see to it, sir. Is the patient already in the hospital?'

'Yes, I got him in last night. Shall I be treading on anyone's toes if I take over theatre at short notice?'

Rachel tried to forget her aching head and thought hard. 'No, we can manage. Norah can take the second theatre—it's Mr Sims tomorrow morning and Mr Jolly in the afternoon. I'll have Staff Nurse Pepys here with me . . .'

She caught George's eloquent eye—he disliked Mrs Pepys and Billy was terrified of her, so she added soothingly, 'If you need to operate between eight o'clock and seven in the morning, Professor, there will be the night staff nurse and the runner as well. They're both very good.'

'Sorry to spring it on you, Rachel.' He sounded quite sincere and he seldom addressed her by her Christian name while they were working. 'There's always a silver lining though; I'll be away for a couple of weeks.'

She said, 'Oh, will you, sir?' rather blankly. It was her headache which made her feel so depressed, she supposed.

She took a Panadol with her coffee presently and her head cleared, so that the rest of the list passed off smoothly enough even though they finished late. The Professor might be a stickler for punctuality, she reflected, going down to a warmed-up dinner, but he forgot that there was such a thing as time once he was scrubbed.

The afternoon list with the fourth consultant, Mr Reeves, an elderly man on the verge of retirement, went well. Rachel handed over to Norah just after five o'clock, and went off duty. An early night, she told herself, trying to ignore the hope that Melville would phone her. A quiet evening somewhere, perhaps outside London, where they could have a meal and talk without the constant greetings and interruptions from his friends. Rachel sighed as she got out of her uniform and pottered off to look for an empty bathroom.

But he didn't phone; she took a long time changing into a knitted suit and then, unwilling to spend an evening in the sitting-room with the other sisters, thrust some money into a purse, and went down to the entrance. She wasn't at all sure what she was going to do—perhaps a run in the car . . .

She was getting out her car key when Professor van Teule loomed up beside her. 'Ah,' he said sleepily. 'Going out, Rachel?'

'Yes—no. I don't know,' she almost snapped at him. 'I just want to get away for an hour.' She added by way of explanation, 'It's a nice evening.'

He took the key from her in his large hand, picked up her purse from the car's bonnet where she had laid it, and put the key into it.

'You sound undecided. Moreover, you don't look in a fit state to drive a car. I'm going for a quiet potter— why not come with me? We can eat somewhere quiet and you can doze off in peace.'

She had to laugh. 'It's kind of you to suggest it, Professor, but I couldn't go to sleep; it would be rude . . . '

'Not with me, it wouldn't. You need a nap badly, Rachel. You're wound up too tightly; don't you know that? No sign of, er, Melville?'

'You always say "er, Melville", as though you can't remember his name,' she said crossly.

'Well, I can't.' He sounded reasonable. Really, it was impossible to be put out by him.

'He's a very busy man.'

The Professor, hardly idle himself, nodded understandingly. 'If you had a quiet evening out of town, you'd be as fresh as a daisy in the morning and ready to go dancing again when he asks you.'

She stood looking up at him. He was kind and friendly in an impersonal way and it sounded tempting, to be driven into the country for an hour.

She asked abruptly, 'Why do you ask me?'

'You run the theatre block very efficiently, Rachel, and to do that you have to be one hundred per cent fit; my motive is purely selfish, you see.'

She found that his answer disappointed her. 'Well, thank you, I'll come, only I would like an early night.'

'Don't worry, I'll see that you're back by ten o'clock at the latest. I shall want to take a quick look at that young man later on, anyway.'

The Rolls was ultra-comfortable; she sat back with an unconscious sigh and the professor suggested, 'Why not close your eyes until we're clear of London? I'll wake you once there is something worth seeing.'

'Don't you like London?' she asked. Somehow she had pictured him, when she had bothered to think about him at all, as a man about town, wining and dining and going to the theatre; having smart friends.

'No. Close your eyes, Rachel.'

She closed them and, although she hadn't meant to, went to sleep at once.

He had turned off the motorway at Maidenhead before he woke her up.

'There's rather a nice pub by the river at Moulsford—the Beetle and Wedge—we'll bypass Henley and go across country. It's charming scenery and it's still light.'

Rachel, much refreshed by her nap, sat up. 'Sorry I went to sleep, but I feel fine now.'

'Good. I hope you're hungry—I am.'

He talked easily as they drove through the country roads and after a while arrived at the Beetle and Wedge. It was an old inn surrounded by trees and with plenty of garden around it. And it was cosy and welcoming inside. They sat by the log fire in the bar and had leisurely drinks and then dined generously; here they hadn't heard of *crudités*. There was watercress soup with a lavish spoonful of cream atop, followed by steak and kidney pie which melted in the mouth, and even more generous portions of vegetables. Rachel polished off the home-made ice cream she had chosen and drank the last of the claret the Professor had ordered—a very nice wine, she had observed, and he had agreed gravely; a vintage 1981 Château Léoville-Lascases should be nice. He had no doubt that she would be thunderstruck if she knew what it cost.

They had coffee round the fire in the pleasantly filled bar and, true to his word, when she suggested rather diffidently that she would like an early night, he got up at once, paid the bill and settled her in the car. This time he took the main road through Henley and then on to Maidenhead and the motorway, so that they were back at the hospital minutes before ten o'clock.

It was unfortunate, to say the least of it, that Melville should have been getting into his car as Rachel got out of the Professor's.

The Professor shut the car door behind her and she heard him say, 'Oh, dear, dear,' in an infuriatingly mild voice. She felt his reassuring bulk behind her as Melville left his car and came towards them.

'Rachel? I came to take you out for a drink.' He smiled but his eyes were angry. 'But I see that someone else had the same idea.' He gave the Professor an angry look.

'Ah, Mr-er-Grant, isn't it? Good evening. My dear fellow, how vexing for you. We have been for a run into the country. Rachel has had a busy day and so have I. We return considerably refreshed.' He smiled gently and made no move to go away.

Rachel touched Melville on his coat sleeve. 'Melville, I'm so sorry to have missed you. You didn't phone— I had no idea.'

'You're not the only one who's had a busy day.' Melville's voice held a sneer. 'Well, I'll be on my way— I'll see you some time.'

He was going, probably out of her life for ever. Rachel swallowed panic. 'Melville, I've said I'm sorry. If only you had let me know . . . Can't we go somewhere and have a drink now?'

'I left a desk full of work to come and see you.' declared Melville dramatically. 'I'll go back and finish it.'

'Look, can't we talk?' asked Rachel desperately and glanced round at the Professor, hoping that he might take the hint and leave them alone. He returned her look with a placid one of his own and she saw that he had no intention of doing that. There he stood, saying nothing, silently watching and not being of the least help. She said again, 'Melville . . . ' but that gentleman turned without another word and went back to his car, got in and drove away.

'He'll ruin that engine,' observed the Professor, 'crashing his gears like that.'

'Who cares about his gears?' asked Rachel wildly. 'He's gone and I don't suppose he'll ever come back.'

'Oh, yes he will, Rachel. There is nothing like a little healthy competition to keep a man interested; something which I'm sure you know already. Not, I must hasten to add, that in fact there is competition, but, there is no harm in letting, er, Melville think so.'

'Don't be absurd,' snapped Rachel, and then, 'Do you really think so? You don't think he's gone forever?'

Her voice shook a little at the idea.

He was reassuringly matter-of-fact. 'Most certainly not. Men want the unobtainable, and you were unobtainable this evening—you are a challenge to his vanity.' He sighed. 'You don't know much about men, do you, Rachel?'

She said indignantly, 'I have three brothers . . . '

'That isn't quite what I meant. I dare say you boss them about most dreadfully and take them for granted like an old coat.'

She stared up at him. 'Well, yes, perhaps. But Melville's different.'

'Indeed he is.' His sleepy eyes searched her face. 'You love him very much, do you not?' He added, *'pro tempore,'* which, since she wasn't listening properly, meant nothing to her; in any case her knowledge of Latin was confined to medical terms.

'Go to bed, Rachel.' His voice was comfortably avuncular. 'In the morning you'll think straight again. Only believe me when I say that your Melville hasn't gone for good.'

She whispered, 'You're awfully kind,' then added, to her own astonishment as well as his, 'Are you married, Professor?'

'That is a pleasure I still have to experience within the not too distant future. Run along, there's a good girl.'

Emotion and the Château Léoville-Lascases got the better of her good sense. She stood on tiptoe and kissed his cheek and then ran into the hospital.

She felt terrible about it in the morning; thank heaven he had no list, she thought as she went on duty. She opened her office door and found him sitting at the desk: immaculate and placid, writing busily.

He glanced up at her. 'Oh, good morning, Sister. Can you fit in an emergency? Multiple abdominal stab wounds—some poor blighter set upon in the small hours. Mr Sims has a list, hasn't he?'

'Not till ten o'clock, sir.' Rachel had forgotten any awkwardness she had been harbouring, for the moment at least. 'I can have theatre ready in fifteen minutes; Mr Sims could do his first case in the second theatre—Norah's on as well as me.'

' "I" ' corrected the Professor. 'Very well, I'll give Mr Sims a ring.' He gave her a casual glance. 'I'll be up in twenty minutes if you can manage that.'

She nodded, rather pink in the face, and left him there to go into theatre and warn her nurses.

It was just as though last night had never been. The Professor duly arrived, dead on time as usual, with George to assist him, exchanged a few friendly remarks of an impersonal nature with her, and got down to work, and when he was done and they were drinking their coffee in her office, he maintained a distant manner that vaguely disquieted her. She had felt awkward at first, but now she was worried that the calm relationship they had had had been disturbed.

He went presently, thanking her as he always did, and she set about organising the rest of Mr Sims's list, thankful that the transplant had fallen through.

She worried about it all day, feeling guilty because only every now and then did she remember Melville. But once she was off duty, Melville took over. Perhaps he would phone, she reflected, and hurried to shower and change just in case he did and wanted her to go out. But he didn't; she spent a dull evening in the sisters' sitting-room, watching a film she had already seen on TV and listening to Sister Chalk criticising her student nurses. I'll be like that, thought Rachel desperately, unless I marry and get away from here. She said aloud, breaking into Sister Chalk's soliloquy concerning a third-year nurse who had cheeked her only that morning, 'I'm going to bed; I've had a busy day.'

George had a short list in the morning; Rachel left Mrs Pepys to scrub after the first case and went into the office to catch up on the paperwork. She hadn't been there ten minutes when the phone rang. It was Melville. She had made it plain when they had first met that he must never ring her during duty hours and she felt a small spurt of annoyance because he had ignored that, but it was quickly swept away with the pleasure of hearing his voice.

'Melville . . . ' She tried to sound severe, but her delight bubbled through. 'I'm on duty—I asked you not to phone when I'm working.'

'I'm working, too, darling Rachel, but I can't concentrate until I've told you what a prize moron I was last night. Put it down to disappointment. Say you forgive me and come out this evening.'

She hoped he hadn't noticed the short pause before she answered. 'Yes' was ready to trip off her tongue when she remembered the Professor's words. Men wanted the unobtainable; OK, she would be just that for this evening at least. She was a poor liar for she always blushed when she was fibbing, but there was no one to see now so that she sounded convincing enough. 'I can't. I know I'm off at five o'clock but they're doing a couple of private patients this evening.'

'The quicker you leave that damned place the better—talk about slavery . . . '

She said reasonable, 'Not really—I shall get my off duty hours made up to me when we're slack.'

'And when will that be?'

'I could get a couple of hours added on to my off duty tomorrow.'

'That'll make it when?' he sounded eager.

'About three o'clock for the rest of the day.'

'I'll be outside at three-thirty. We'll drive some-where and have a quiet dinner.'

'That would be nice. Melville, I must ring off.' And she did. Usually she waited until he had hung up, but the Professor had given her ideas . . .

Since only one theatre was in use for dentals the next morning, Rachel had plenty of time to decide what she would wear. Norah was off duty but she and the second part-time staff nurse would be on again at two o'clock. In the meantime Rachel handed forceps and swabs and mouthwashes and wished that Mr Reed, the dentist, would hurry up. When finally he finished and had been given his coffee it was time for first dinner. She left two student nurse to clean the theatre and went along to the canteen.

It was fish pie, turnips and instant mash; although she was hungry she only half filled her plate. Melville was fussy about his food and always took her somewhere where the cooking was superb.

There were half a dozen of her friends already sharing a table and she joined them, pecking at the wholesome food with such reluctance that Lucy asked her if she was sickening for something.

'Just not hungry,' said Rachel, who was. She filled her empty insides with tea and went back to the theatre. Norah had just come on duty and there was little to do. They planned a wholesale cleaning operation, leaving one theatre free for any emergency which might come in, decided that Mrs Crow, the part-time staff nurse on duty for the afternoon, could scrub for the three cases of tonsillectomy, and conned the next day's list.

By then it was three o'clock; half an hour in which to make the best of herself. Rachel raced through a shower, brushed her hair until it shone, plaited it neatly into a bun again, and went to study the contents of her wardrobe.

It would have to be the suit again, but this time she would wear the pale pink blouse with it. She thrust her feet into high-heeled shoes, found gloves and handbag and, with an anxious eye on the clock, went down to the forecourt. She was a little late and she hadn't yet learned to keep a man waiting; indeed, the reverse, growing up as she had with three brothers.

Melville was waiting and his greeting was everything a girl could wish for; she got into the car beside him feeling on top of the world, and she stayed that way for the rest of the afternoon and evening. He had never been so amusing nor so anxious that she should be enjoying herself. They had tea in Richmond and then drove on through Hampshire and into Wiltshire to stop in Marlborough and dine at the Castle and Ball, a pleasant and comfortable hotel, but not, thought Rachel fleetingly, Melville's usual kind of place in which to eat. As though he had heard her unspoken thought, he said lightly, 'I had thought of going to Marlow—the Compleat Angler—but this place is quiet and the food is good.' His glance strayed over her person making her aware of the suit he had seen several times already.

'I'm not dressed for anything four-star.' She wasn't apologising, only stating a fact. 'This looks very nice.'

That was the only small fly in the ointment. They lingered over the surprisingly good dinner and it was after ten o'clock by the time they got into the car again. It would be midnight before she reached her room and she was on duty in the morning. Not that that mattered; she was so happy she didn't give it a second thought.

Melville drove back to London very fast, not saying much. He was tired, she decided, and so said little herself. They were back before midnight and although he kissed her and declared that he had enjoyed every minute of it, he made no effort to delay her; indeed, he leaned across and opened her door with the remark that he would see her just as soon as he could, and drove away before she could do more than utter the most cursory of thanks.

The poor dear, she found herself reflecting as she went inside, he works too hard. Professor van Teule was crossing the entrance hall; Melville wasn't the only one to work hard, but she didn't dwell on that, she would have found it strange if the Professor hadn't. Come to that, she worked hard herself, but she didn't dwell on that; either. She was remembering the delights of the evening and turned a smiling face to him as their paths crossed. She wished him goodnight in a cheerful voice and he answered her with his usual courtesy, glancing with deceptive sleepiness at her happy face. The night porter wondered why he should look so thoughtful as he went out to his car.

Rachel didn't see him the next day; Mr Jolly had a list and Mr Reeves had the second theatre in the afternoon. She went off duty at five o'clock after a routine day, changed and went to the local cinema with two of her friends. It was a tatty place but showed surprisingly good films, and strangely enough although the neighbourhood was prone to muggings and petty thieving, the staff of the hospital, even out of uniform, were treated with respect. They had coffee and sandwiches at Ned's café, opposite the cinema, and went back to make tea and gossip over it until they decided to go to bed.

Norah had days off and Rachel, going on duty in the morning, remembered with a sigh that Mrs Pepys would be on duty from nine o'clock until three in the afternoon, which meant that the student nurses would be in a state of rebellion by teatime. She could hardly blame them; Mrs Pepys was tiresome at the best of times and not of much use, for the Professor had indicated months ago in the nicest possible way that he preferred not to have her scrub for him. There were three heavy cases and he would be doing them all, which meant that Mrs Pepys would be left with the afternoon dentals and laying up between cases, two tasks she felt too superior to undertake.

She would do them, of course; Rachel had a quiet authority which made itself felt upon occasion.

She checked the theatres, gave the student nurses their allotted places and went to scrub. She had laid up the trolleys for the first case when the Professor put his head round the door. His good morning was genial. 'There's a man downstairs I'll have to patch up when he's fit enough—can we add him to the list?'

She wondered what he would say if she said no; something soothing and courteous and the man would arrive in the theatre all the same.

'Certainly, sir. Mrs Pepys will be on at nine o'clock and can take dentals this afternoon so it won't matter if we run late.'

'Norah not here?'

'Days off.'

'Time you had yours, isn't it?'

'When Norah gets back.'

He nodded and his head disappeared and presently, when they were ready for him, he came back with George and Billy beside him. His 'Ready, Sister?' was calmly impersonal and a moment later he was bending over his patient, absorbed in his work.

It was more than two hours before the patient was wheeled away.

'Coffee?' asked the Professor, straightening his great back, and, without waiting for an answer, he wandered out of the theatre.

Mrs Pepys was on duty by now. Rachel left her to lay up for the next case, sent two of the nurses to their coffee and repaired to her office. Dolly had carried in the coffee tray and the four men were crowded into the small room, waiting for her. She handed them their mugs, took the lid off the biscuit tin and put it on the table where everyone could reach it. They devoured biscuits as though they were famished and she made a mental note to supplement the meagre supply she was allowed from stores with a few packets of her own.

They drank and munched in a pleasant atmosphere of cameraderie, and the talk was of the patient who had just gone to the recovery room and the next case. Dolly came to refill the coffee pot and Rachel slipped away to see what was going on in theatre. The student nurses were back from their coffee and she sent the third, junior nurse to the canteen and suggested that Mrs Pepys should go at the same time. 'And when you get back will you get ready for dentals?' suggested Rachel. 'There's an extra case coming up and we shall be late. Mr Reed's got three patients—you'll be ready well before three o'clock, so clear up as far as you can, will you? I'll need all the nurses I've got as well as Sidney.'

Mrs Pepys gave her a cross look. 'If you say so, Sister.' She flounced away and Rachel turned back towards the theatre to find the Professor standing behind her. She had let out a gusty sigh and he asked, 'Is she a trouble to you, Rachel? Shall I get her moved?'

She looked at him in surprise. 'She's annoying, sir, but she does her work—I've no good reason for her to be moved. It's only her manner.'

'She scares the little nurses, does she not?'

That surprised her, too; she hadn't credited him with noticing that. 'Yes, but I make sure they come to no harm. It's nice of you to notice, though.'

He turned away. 'Well, let me know if you need help at any time.' And, over his shoulder as he went, 'Are you going home for your days off?'

She felt herself blushing, which was silly. 'I—I don't know. It depends . . . '

'Ah, yes—Melville, of course.'

They didn't talk again that day, only to exchange necessary words about the patients or the instruments he needed. The list finished in the early afternoon and he went away at once, wishing her his usual placid goodbye. For some reason she felt put out, although she was unable to decide quite why that should be. Something was happening to their former easygoing relationship and she had no idea what it was.

CHAPTER THREE

RACHEL forgot her vague disquiet almost at once. For one thing there was the usual upset between Mrs Pepys and one of the student nurses to settle and then, at tea time, an emergency appendix which George did. She went off duty debating as to whether she should go home or stay in the hope that Melville would call her with some plan of his own. He hadn't mentioned seeing her on her days off, but he seldom planned anything in advance. Too busy, she thought fondly. It took her only a few moments to decide to stay, certain that Melville would ring; he knew that she had days off, she had told him and he had said that they must spend them together.

She sat in the sitting-room for an hour, willing the telephone to ring, but, since it hadn't by supper time, she went to the canteen and then, refusing offers to go to the cinema with some of her friends, she went to her room and washed her hair, a long business because of its length and thickness. She followed this by doing her nails and examining her pretty face, searching for signs of wrinkles. Finally, she went to bed. Melville would surely phone in the morning; she slept peacefully on the thought.

She got her own breakfast in the pantry at the end of the sisters' corridor and dressed with care. It was a cold blustery morning, quite suitable for the wearing of her winter coat, recently bought and fashionable and which would allow her to wear a silk jersey dress, so that if they stayed out to dinner she would look all right. She perched a little angora cap on to her braided topknot, and, gloves and bag in her hand, went down to the entrance hall. She was so certain that Melville would have written to her that she didn't hesitate, but went straight to the porter's lodge for her post.

There were several letters for her but only one which mattered. She opened it quickly, vaguely aware that it had been delivered by hand, and read it, and then read it again. Melville knew that she would understand; an American actress had joined the cast of the production he was working on and he had been asked to show her something of London; he had intended telling her on the previous evening but there had been a drinks party which had lasted rather a long while. Lucky that they hadn't had anything planned and he would give her a ring early in the week. He had no doubt that she would have a super couple of days off.

Her instant rage was swallowed up in a wave of unhappiness. He could have told her earlier so that she could have gone home. Now half a day at least had been wasted, for she could have driven down on the previous evening. Here she was, dressed for a smart restaurant and probably a theatre with Melville, who took it for granted that she would understand. She had been silly, she admitted to herself, to expect a man as important as Melville to be free to come and go as he wished, and sillier still to have been so sure of him. She read the letter once again and took comfort from the endearments which strewed it so liberally. He must love her very much to write like that . . . She became aware of someone standing beside her—Professor van Teule, calmly and unforgivably reading the letter she had still open in her hand.

'Oh, bad luck,' he said placidly, and smiled so kindly that the heated words on her tongue were unuttered. All she said was rather weakly, 'You have no right . . . '

'None,' he agreed cheerfully, 'but how very fortunate that I should, er, glimpse the contents of your letter. I am about to drive down to Bath and will be glad to give you a lift.'

'But I live miles from there.' She knew that she sounded ungracious, but disappointment was still biting deep.

'I had intended to take the road through Andover, and I seem to remember you telling me at some time or other that you lived in that part of the world.'

If she hadn't been quite so upset she would have remembered nothing of the sort. As it was, she mumbled, 'I told Mother yesterday evening that I was going to stay here . . . '

The Professor became all at once very brisk. 'Give her a ring now.' His glance took in her little cap and high-heeled shoes. 'I need ten minutes to talk to George; you can change if you want and meet me here.'

He propelled her gently towards the porter's lodge, but as she was lifting the receiver she said hesitantly, 'We're not allowed to use this phone.'

'Leave that to me.' He turned his back and engaged the head porter in conversation as she dialled her home number.

Her mother answered the phone. 'Now isn't that nice?' she commented. 'Your brothers are home—we'll have a cosy weekend together. Are you driving, darling?'

Rachel explained. 'Oh, good.' Mrs Downing's voice was casual in the extreme. 'You'll be here before lunch. Will he stay, this Professor?'

'Most unlikely—he's going on to Bath.'

She put down the receiver and saw that the Professor was still deep in conversation with Simkins, the elderly head porter, who, if rumour had it right, had been there ever since Victorian times. She went towards them now and the Professor turned his head to ask, 'All right? Good, ten minutes then.'

She went back to her room and changed into a sweater and skirt and a quilted jacket, rammed a few necessities into an overnight bag, got into a pair of sturdy shoes, and hurried back to the entrance hall. The Professor was there, talking to George, who gave her a friendly grin and then walked to the entrance with them both.

'Goodbye, sir. I'll see what I can find you when you get back. Rachel, don't forget it's take-in next week.'

He laughed and raised a hand as the Professor took the Rolls smoothly out into the traffic, joining the steady stream going west.

He had little to say, and that required little in the way of a reply, something which was a relief to Rachel, busy with her thoughts about Melville. They gained the motorway and the Professor put his large, elegantly shod foot down so that the car ate up the miles, but once they were off the motorway he slowed the car and presently stopped at a wayside café.

'Shall we have coffee? We've made good time.'

'Yes, please. But have you to be in Bath for lunch? You'll be late if you take me home first.'

'There is time enough,' he told her in his unhurried way, and for some reason she felt snubbed. Over their coffee she made small talk, feeling guilty because for such a lot of the journey she had said almost nothing. As they got back into the car she tried to put that right. 'I'm sorry I'm such a dull companion, but I wanted to think . . . '

'Let us say restful rather than dull. And I had the opportunity to think a few thoughts of my own, Rachel.'

Which made her uneasy. Was he hinting that he wanted to stay silent for the rest of the journey, or just being kind?

She played safe and kept quiet, and discovered that their silence was a friendly one. There was no need to make conversation; she felt quite as ease, and so, apparently, did the Professor.

As he drew up before her home it struck her that he hadn't hesitated once on the way, nor had she given him any directions; she was on the point of pointing this interesting fact out to him when her mother opened the door and came out to the car.

Mrs Downing wasn't in the least like her daughter. She was barely middle height, plump, but pretty still, looking incapable of running a house, let alone helping her husband, cooking meals at odd hours, waiting with endless patience for him to come home, and owning three very large sons and a daughter, who if not large, was a good deal taller than herself.

She poked her head through the window the Professor had opened and beamed at them both. 'Darling, how nice. Your brothers are in the kitchen.' She turned still-beautiful blue eyes upon the professor and Rachel said quickly, 'This is Professor van Teule, Mother; he kindly gave me a lift.'

Mrs Downing offered a hand. 'I've often wondered what you were like,' she told him chattily. 'Not a bit what I expected. Will you stay for lunch?'

He smiled at her. 'You are most kind to ask me, but I have to get to Bath.'

'Charming place, have you friends there?' She didn't wait for him to answer. 'Are you calling to take Rachel back tomorrow?'

Rachel pinkened and frowned and the Professor's eyes gleamed with amusement.

'Certainly.' He turned to look at Rachel. 'About eight o'clock?' he asked.

'You'll have to come out of your way.'

'A few miles. Eight o'clock, Rachel?'

She scowled at him, wishing she could refuse the lift her mother had angled for. She said crossly, 'Very well, Professor, thank you.'

'There'll be coffee for you,' said Mrs Downing happily. 'My husband will be delighted to meet you.'

The Professor replied suitably, bade Mrs Downing goodbye, said nonchalantly to Rachel, 'Tomorrow evening, then,' and drove off.

'What a very nice man,' said Mrs Downing, leading the way indoors. 'Is he married? No? Going to be? What a pity, he would suit you down to the ground, darling. And you told me you'd never really looked at him. How could you not? Such a handsome man . . .'

Rachel put an arm round her parent. 'Mother,' she said patiently, 'the Professor is someone I work for. We get on well enough, but I don't know anything about him and he doesn't know anything about me.'

'He knows where you live,' said Mrs Downing happily.

No one mentioned Melville until Sunday morning, on the way to church, when Mrs Downing asked casually if he was in London. 'For these important men do get around, don't they?' she added chattily.

'He's having to show some American actress the sights this weekend,' said Rachel shortly, 'and he's very busy.' She added defensively, 'We had a lovely afternoon and evening out last week.'

She was glad that her three brothers joined them then and there was no need to say more.

Sunday passed peacefully; church, one of Mrs Downing's superbly cooked lunches and then a long lazy afternoon sitting round the fire in the comfortable, rather shabby drawing-room, with the Sunday papers strewn all over the place and desultory family gossip. They had supper early since Rachel was leaving that evening, and the meal had been cleared away before the Professor arrived, exactly at eight o'clock. Rachel was ready to go but he seemed in no hurry; he accepted her mother's invitation to have coffee and followed her into the drawing-room, where her father and three brothers subjected him to a brief scrutiny as she introduced him. They seemed to like what they saw; over coffee and one of her mother's ginger cakes, the men talked and it was almost nine o'clock when, at last, the Professor asked her, 'Well, are you ready, Rachel?' A remark which she considered most unfair, since she had been ready for an hour.

It took another fifteen minutes to say goodbye to everyone and, to make matters worse, the Professor made no attempt to drive fast. Perhaps Melville had phoned, she thought distractedly, and she hadn't been there—he might have written or called . . . she'd been a fool to go home.

Her companion, uncannily reading her thoughts, observed placidly, 'Well, let us hope that, er, Melville has phoned or called to take you out.'

'Of all the nasty unkind things to say,' began Rachel fiercely.

'No, no you mistake me. Can you not see that his appetite will be whetted? The unobtainable, Rachel—that is what you have to be,' he added with tiresome conviction. 'Use your wits, girl.'

Rachel almost choked with temper. 'Well!' She paused to think up a scathing remark, and he laughed and said, 'What a pity you don't treat, er, Melville to one of your bad tempers.' His voice changed from mockery to avuncular kindness. 'Rachel, if you want him you'll need to fight for him.' He sighed soundlessly. 'You have the weapons: youth and beauty and a pretty voice and, besides these, a good brain and plenty of common sense.' He was silent for a few moments. 'Don't try and be what he thinks you should be; be yourself—if he loves you he won't care if he takes you out wearing a potato sack.'

'You're full of good advice,' she said bitterly.

'I do my best,' he told her placidly. 'Have you had supper?'

'Ages ago.'

'Good, then we could stop for a sandwich. It will give me an opportunity to discuss tomorrow's list—I want to make some alterations. I shall be away for a couple of weeks; George will cope, but there's a case I want transferred and added . . . can we do that?'

He had become Professor van Teule again, impersonal and friendly, with his mind on his work. They stopped at a service station and drank some awful coffee and ate sandwiches which looked and tasted as though they were made of plastic, and talked shop the whole time.

The Professor wasn't a man to leave a girl to open her own door, even if it was only the hospital entrance; he took her overnight bag and saw her into the entrance hall, but before she could say goodbye the night porter poked his head out of his cubby hole.

'There's a phone call for you, Sister. I was just ringing round for you.'

'Melville,' uttered the Professor and gave her a little push towards the porter's lodge. 'Take it here and remember what I said.'

It was indeed Melville. Where had she been? He had called twice already. 'I've missed you so,' he added plaintively.

She was on the point of saying that she'd missed him, too, when she remembered the Professor's advice. She said in rather a cold voice, 'I've been home for the weekend. Just this minute got in.'

'I'll be round in ten minutes—we can go to my club and have a drink.'

It cost her a lot to say lightly, 'Sorry, Melville, I'm on my way to bed. There's an early list in the morning and I'll be needing all my wits.'

What was more, she hung up on him.

'Oh, splendid!' The Professor's quiet voice made her jump; she hadn't known that he was right behind her. Probably he had heard every word. He was, she reflected, quite unscrupulous.

'You have him in the hollow of your hand,' he said. 'Goodnight Rachel.'

He had gone, while she was still gaping at him.

There was, indeed, a heavy list in the morning; Professor van Teule, since he would be away for two weeks, was intent on getting as much work done as possible before he went. Rachel, after a sound night's sleep despite her doubts as to whether she hadn't been a bit drastic in her treatment of Melville, went calmly through her day. The Professor's list extended far beyond its time limits; they stopped briefly between cases to snatch a cup of coffee and a sandwich and then went on again, with the faithful Norah laying up each fresh case and Rachel scrubbing. It was a blessing that Mrs Pepys wasn't on duty; the routine went smoothly and the student nurses, even the junior one, were lulled into a state of instant obedience and confidence by the Professor's pleasantly casual manner and Rachel's unflappable demeanour.

It was almost three o'clock by the time they had finished his last case and Rachel thanked heaven that Mr Jolly had phoned in to say that he was cancelling his list because he had a heavy cold. Norah, who had gone off duty for the afternoon, came on again at six o'clock, and Rachel, bogged down in paperwork, hailed her with relief. 'What a day! We finished at three o'clock and it took us all of two hours to clear and clean. I've almost finished here. You've got Nurse Walters on. There's nothing in the accident room, so with luck you'll have a quiet evening.'

'Has he gone?' asked Norah.

'Not until the morning,' observed the Professor from the doorway. And, as they turned to look at him, 'Don't worry, I don't want to operate. That last case, I didn't write up the notes. If I might trouble you . . . '

Rachel got up. 'Sit here, sir. I'm going off duty. Norah will be in theatre if you need anything.'

She found the case book he wanted and laid it ready on the desk. 'I hope you have a pleasant holiday,' she said politely.

'Thank you.' He sat down at the desk and pulled the notes towards him and she had the unpleasant sensation of being shut out. She bade him goodbye in a cold voice, cast a speaking glance at Norah and left the office.

There was no phone call from Melville. Rachel spent the evening in the sitting-room, knitting a complicated sweater which should have taken all her attention but didn't, so that she unpicked almost as much as she knitted. Perhaps she had been too harsh with Melville; perhaps the Professor's advice hadn't been all that good. She pondered the matter at length, giving absent-minded answers to her friends' remarks, not really hearing them.

When she went to bed she was still thinking about it, so that it was all the more surprising that her last thoughts were of the Professor. Where did he go when he went on holiday? she wondered. To Holland? To stay with the girl he was going to marry? Did he have parents like everyone else? And where did they live? These questions and others quite ousted Melville from her mind.

She had to admit after a day or two that she missed the Professor; at least, she missed the bustle and urgency of working for him. George had lists, of course, and so did Mr Jolly and Mr Reeves, and of course there were the dental cases, but, whereas the Professor always worked himself and everyone else to their capacity, the days were now orderly, with everyone going off duty at the right time and the lists finishing exactly when they should. So that, when

Melville at last phoned, she was in a mood to agree with anything he might suggest.

A party, he told her; the production he had been busy with had been completed, and they were having a celebration. He would fetch her at nine o'clock the next evening, and she was to wear her prettiest dress. 'I missed you, darling,' he declared. 'It seems ages since I saw you. Thank heaven I'll have nothing important on for a time—we'll see each other as much as possible.' He added dramatically, 'You have no idea how busy I've been.'

Rachel had been busy, too, but she was too happy to say so. Perhaps after all the Professor's advice was bearing fruit.

She gave a good deal of thought to what she was going to wear. She was off duty at six, which gave her ample time in which to change her mind half a dozen times. The women would be smart; more than that, they would be fashionable and expensively dressed and she mustn't let Melville down. She decided on a long black skirt, a vividly patterned silk top which had cost the earth and a wide black satin sash of Lucy's. Not bad, she considered, inspecting her reflection and admiring the black satin slippers she had bought for their last evening out. She had a long black evening cloak which seemed too dramatic for the occasion and Lucy came to the rescue once more with the offer of her short fur jacket: rabbit, and a little on the small side, but it lent a certain cachet to the outfit.

Remembering the Professor's advice again she waited until five minutes past the hour before going down to the entrance; she found Melville waiting for her in his car. He didn't get out but opened the door for her and kissed her warmly when she got in. 'Darling, you're more beautiful than ever. How I've longed to see you. This is going to be some party—in Chelsea—everyone who's anyone will be there.'

Rachel said, 'Oh, how nice,' feeling this to be an inadequate remark, but Melville wasn't listening; he was reciting names to her—important names of the important people they would meet. It took the entire drive to complete and left Rachel, who wasn't at all up-to-date with the latest pop stars, bewildered.

The party was being held in a large terraced house near the river; there were rows of cars in the street outside and lights blazing from every window. 'Hurry up,' begged Melville and leaned across to open the door impatiently.

The house inside was opulent and very warm. It was also brilliantly lit and the huge chandelier in the hall shone down on the rabbit so that there was no hope of passing it off as anything else. Melville gave it a look as she handed it to a haughty-looking maid, then he cast an eye over her person. 'I don't suppose you had time to buy something more suitable,' he began, and then paused at the look Rachel gave him. 'Not that you don't look smashing,' he added hastily. 'You always look marvellous. Let's go in.'

The room they entered was packed and the noise of voices drowned normal speech. Melville seemed to know everyone as he made his way across the room with Rachel close beside him. At the far end standing by a roaring fire was their host, or so she presumed; it was impossible to hear what Melville was saying. She shook hands and smiled and accepted a glass of something and to her dismay saw Melville disappear into a group of people standing nearby. She sipped the drink which she privately decided was sugared petrol, and then looked around her. The women's dresses were fabulous; she stuck out like a sore thumb and her hair was all wrong. Several of the girls there had brightly coloured hair—pink and purple and pale blue and even the normal colours had been coaxed into wild clouds of crimped hair, or spikey hairdos, and there were several with hair so short and sleek that it seemed to have been painted on to their heads. Rachel stood there, entertaining wild ideas about having her hair cut off and buying some shoes with diamond encrusted heels three inches high at least, and was roused from these unlikely happenings by a pleasant voice at her elbow.

'You came with Melville Grant, didn't you? You're his latest girl, aren't you? We've all been wondering what you were like! A smasher, I can see that. But then he always has the best.'

Rachel turned to look at the speaker; if the words had been offensive she was sure that they weren't intended to be. The middle-aged woman beside her had a kind and smiling face, motherly in fact, and was dressed in the kind of frock that one would expect a middle-aged woman to wear. Moreover, her hair was frankly streaked with grey and twisted untidily into a small bun.

'I'm Pat Morris—I write TV scripts and try to do a bit of directing too. Work sometimes with Melville; that's how I got to hear about you.'

She put out a hand and Rachel took it. 'How do you do,' she said politely. 'I'm Rachel Downing and yes, I came with Melville.' She decided to ignore the rest of her companion's remarks. A handsome, sought-after man such as Melville would naturally enough have lots of girlfriends, but they had to come to an end one day and he had told her on numerous occasions that she was the only girl in the world for him. She glanced across the room to where he stood surrounded by a laughing group of people and Pat Morris followed her gaze. 'Always the life and soul of any party,' she commented. 'I don't know how he does it, though his work isn't all that demanding. He's got a secretary, of course, and an assistant, and he doesn't have to work till all hours like some of us.' She took a sip from the glass she was holding, and pulled a face. 'Poison.' she said and went on chattily, 'Away at half-past four every day and not a sign of him until ten o'clock the next morning.'

Rachel said, 'Oh, yes,' in a doubtful voice. Why had Melville told her that he worked far into the night, and, if he didn't, where did he go and what did he do? Something she would ask him.

They were joined presently by a youngish man in horn-rimmed glasses and a thin woman in black draperies and rows and rows of beads. They were introduced as Fay and Murphy and embarked at once on a commentary of the people at the party. Rachel stood and listened. There was no need to say anything; when Fay paused for breath Murphy carried on, cheerfully slandering everyone in sight. They told her, laughing heartily, that they wouldn't say anything about Melville and she said gently, 'Well, I don't suppose there's anything much to say,' which remark left them for the moment speechless.

There was an awkward little silence after that broken by someone offering them tiny sandwiches on a tray. Rachel could have eaten the lot and was horrified when they were waved away by her companions. 'I simply can't eat after dinner,' said Pat and Fay added, 'Food can be such a bore.' She looked at Rachel's nicely shaped person. 'You'll put on weight,' she pointed out, 'eating between meals. As it is you'd photograph on the plump side.'

Rachel decided not to mention that her last meal had been at midday and the next would be breakfast. She said mildly, 'Well, no one photographs me, so I'm not worried.'

'You exercise?' asked Murphy.

'Quite strenuously,' said Rachel gravely.

They were joined by another three persons who were hailed with shrieks of laughter and enquiries as to whether they had had their licenses endorsed. A slight accident with their car, explained Murphy rapidly. No one hurt; at least, the driver of the other car had a leg broken, or it could have been an arm, he wasn't sure. But wasn't it a huge joke?

Rachel, a forthright girl, would have had quite a lot to say about that but it struck her forcibly that these people would stare at her uncomprehendingly and label her a prig, and what good would it do anyway? She couldn't get a word in edgeways as it was and besides, she had to think of Melville . . .

He joined them a moment later, putting a careless arm around her shoulders. 'And how's my girl?' he wanted to know. 'Having a splendid time, I can see that. Have another drink. Toss that one off, darling, and I'll get you something else.'

She handed him her glass. 'No thanks, Melville, it's almost midnight. I must go, but you don't have to come. Could you get a taxi for me?'

'My dear girl, you can't possibly leave yet. Why, the evening is only just beginning.'

She sensed his annoyance and she almost gave in, but the Professor's advice was still loud in her ear. 'Perhaps it is for you,' she told him cheerfully, 'but I'm a working girl.' She gave him a bewitching smile, nodded to Pat and Murphy and Fay without looking to see if he was following her and made her way to where her host was standing.

She made her farewells charmingly so that he looked after her as she went out of the room and observed to the man standing with him. 'How refreshing to meet a girl like that—I'd forgotten they existed.'

Rachel had a moment of panic when she realised that Melville wasn't going to drive her home, but his explanation was plausible enough, and she, hopelessly infatuated, was ready to accept it and make excuses for him besides. He couldn't leave the party, he explained as they stood in the hall waiting for her taxi. There were important people there he had to meet, to keep in with; it was part of his job. He kissed her with practised charm and put her into the taxi and paid her fare before he stood back on to the pavement with a final wave. It was only as she reached the hospital that she remembered that he hadn't said anything about their next meeting.

It had been a successful evening on the whole; she felt a little uneasy about the people she had met, but perhaps not all Melville's friends were like that; he must have a family, although he never mentioned them, and some kind of home life. She undressed slowly, in a daydream where she lived with him in a charming house in the country with a brood of children and a clutter of animals. The unlikelihood of this didn't strike her at all, and she got into bed and went to sleep, still with a head full of foolish fantasies.

There were flowers for her the next day, with a card: 'My undying love,' tied to them. They had been delivered to her office and she stuck them in a large jug until she could take them to her room at dinner time.

George and Billy both stared and George said, 'He must love you, Rachel; there's half a week's salary there,' and Mr Jolly when he arrived to take his list let out a low whistle. 'My, my—do I smell romance in the air? Rachel, who's the lucky man?'

She blushed. 'They're just flowers from someone I know,' she observed and made haste to get him interested in the first case.

The week wound to its close and, since it was her weekend off, she decided to go home. Melville hadn't phoned or written and even if he did she wouldn't change her mind. She packed her overnight bag, got into sweater and skirt and went down to her car. On the way she looked to see if there were any letters for her. There was one, from Melville. He would call for her that afternoon—there was a preview he knew she would love.

It needed all her resolution not to dash back to her room and unpack her bag. Instead, she went over to the porter on duty. 'If a Mr Melville Grant calls or comes for me, will you tell him that I've gone home for the weekend please?' She hesitated. 'You won't forget, will you?'

'No, Sister. Shall I say when you'll be back?'

'No, no need. I'm not sure myself and I can always telephone.'

She worried as she drove home; Melville might be so annoyed that he wouldn't want to see her again; perhaps she had been too severe—if things went wrong she would never forgive Professor van Teule and his advice.

Common sense took over as she neared her home. Nothing could be gained by worrying so she would forget about it and enjoy her weekend. Which, surprisingly, she did, helping her mother round the house, driving her father to a couple of urgent cases, taking Mutt the elderly labrador for walks.

The hospital looked unwelcoming as she drove the Fiat round to the car park on her return. The thought went through her head that the week ahead would be dull, for the Professor wouldn't be back for another seven days. There was plenty of work but no transplants or complicated surgery; she was a girl who liked a challenge.

There was a letter for her. Melville was disappointed; he had planned a marvellous time for them both and why couldn't she have let him know that she was going to be away? He had spent a wretched lonely weekend, working late into the night. Which reminded her of what Pat had told her. Did he really work so hard? Probably at home, she told herself. She longed to phone him, but stopped herself in time; it seemed likely that the Professor, who, after all, must have had some experience in such matters, had been right.

The week passed uneventfully and, as sometimes happened, there were few emergencies. Rachel saw Norah off for her weekend and settled down to two days of catching up with paperwork, browsing over catalogues of instruments and teaching student nurses. Melville telephoned her on the Saturday and, since Mrs Pepys was relieving her on the following afternoon, she agreed on meeting him for tea on Sunday. 'But I must be back here by five o'clock,' she warned him, 'so that the staff nurse can go off duty—she's part-time and has a home to run.'

He had sounded eager to see her. The moment Mrs Pepys arrived Rachel hurried to change and then made herself wait so that she wouldn't be too punctual. It was hard when she wanted to spend every second she could with Melville, but she managed it and was rewarded by a warmth she hadn't expected. He drove her to Green Park, and they walked for an hour before having tea in a small, elegant tea-room. He was full of a new series being prepared for television. 'We'll have to go on location,' he explained, 'but not yet. There are weeks of studio work first. We've signed up that actress I took around a short while ago. She'll be marvellous, and the clothes will be gorgeous.'

Rachel listened eagerly; his life seemed so exciting, even though she wasn't sure that she liked his friends. It didn't occur to her that not once during the afternoon did he ask her about her work or what she had done with her days. Only when he told her that he would be free for a good deal of the following week and had planned all kinds of delights for their benefit did she tell him with real regret that Professor van Teule would be back and it was take-in week.

He scowled at that and muttered something about her loving her work more than him.

'No, I don't!' she protested, 'but I can't come and go as I please.'

'You're tied to that tyrant, Professor van Teule; he's got you under his thumb.'

She was a little bewildered. 'That's ridiculous—he does his work, and I do mine. And I'm not under his thumb; he's most considerate, but if a patient needs surgery then we get on with it. If you had to have an emergency operation and had to wait while they found someone to scrub and get the theatre ready, you wouldn't be best pleased.' She added hotly, 'You're being unreasonable.'

'And you are being a righteous little prig.'

He drove much too fast into the hospital forecourt and the Professor, getting out of his car, raised his eyebrows and then stood watching while Rachel got out of the car and without a backward glance hurried into the hospital. Melville turned the car and drove away just as ferociously.

'Now that is interesting,' observed the Professor softly, and he strolled unhurriedly into the hospital in his turn to wander along to the consultants' room and collect his letters. There was a copy of the morrow's list waiting for him—a formidable one; they would all be busy. He doubted if Rachel would get any off duty. 'And a good thing, too,' he murmured and settled himself to read the first of his letters.

CHAPTER FOUR

BAD temper sustained Rachel as she tore through the hospital and gained her room. She got ready for bed still seething, but once there, doubts came crowding in. Was she really a prig? Just because she liked her work, did that mean to say that she was boring? And did Melville really expect her to walk off duty regardless of whether she was needed in the theatre or not? Supposing he never wanted to see her again? There were all those glamorous women, too . . . She fell asleep at last and dreamed that Melville had gone away and would never come back. It was so vivid that she could think of nothing else while she dressed and ate a sketchy breakfast.

But once on duty she had to abandon these troublesome thoughts and plunge into the day's work. She had already seen the theatre list on Saturday; now it lay on her desk, considerably lengthened, and as she studied it the phone rang: George, ringing from the accident room to say that a woman with internal injuries would need surgery as soon as possible.

'But the Professor is starting at half-past eight and the list is bulging.'

'I know. He's seen her and he wants her up first. How soon can you manage?'

'Fifteen minutes. What kind of injuries?'

'Ruptured spleen, internal haemorrhage for a start. I've warned Men's Surgical to delay the first patient.'

She was replacing the receiver when Professor van Teule walked in. His good morning was genial, the glance he gave her sleepy and brief, but long and intent enough to note her pale face and shadowed eyes.

He said placidly, 'Sorry to get us off to such a bad start, Rachel—I've added a couple of cases to the list, too.'

'I've just seen them, sir. Has the patient been cross-matched? Do you want me to send to the Path Lab?'

'I've asked Lucy to see to that. Put out the pedicle forceps and the clamps, will you. Oh, and the curved compression forceps.' He was lounging against the door so that she had to pause before him on her way out. 'Did you have a pleasant weekend?'

'I was on duty, sir.'

'No time off—hard luck on Melville.'

She said stiffly, 'We were able to spend the afternoon together yesterday. Green Park looks lovely—tulips and hyacinths and all the trees budding.' She added, 'I hope you had a good holiday, sir.'

'Delightful, thank you. No one called me "sir" for two whole weeks.'

She blushed faintly. 'No, well, I suppose not—I mean, if you're not in the hospital there's no need . . . '

'I must remember that.' He stood on one side and opened the door for her.

It was nice to have him back, she reflected, giving quiet instructions to Norah and the nurses, The day bade fair to be chaos before its ending but at least life was never dull. She conferred with Sidney, told Norah to see that the nurses went to their coffee as and when they could be spared, and went off to scrub.

The emergency took a long time. 'Coffee?' asked the Professor mildly, handing over to George and standing away from the table.

Rachel nodded to Nurse Saunders and went on handing things to George and Billy. There was a mass of work ahead of them but the nurses had gone to their coffee, Norah was having hers at that very moment and would lay up for the next case andSidney would be back within minutes. Rachel reviewed the theatre list and thought that, with luck, they might be done by two o'clock.

They weren't, of course; a second emergency—a perforated appendix in a teenage girl had to be squeezed in between the last two cases and, to complicate matters, Mrs Pepys phoned to say that she didn't feel well and wouldn't be coming in for her usual afternoon duty. Which meant that Norah had to go into the second theatre to take Mr Jolly's list, and take two nurses with her.

They had stopped after the fourth case and had a hasty meal of sandwiches and coffee and then gone steadily on, reinforced by Nurse Saunders who had had a long weekend off duty and came on at one o'clock, which mean that the junior nurse could take her time off. Rachel didn't need to worry aboutSidney; he stayed stolidly doing all he was supposed to do and he wouldn't go off duty until he was no longer needed. He was a tower of strength in theatre and liked by everyone; for his part he admired Rachel and considered the Professor to be the finest man he had ever met.

They worked on steadily, in a comfortable friendly atmosphere, until at length the Professor straightened his back for the last time.

'Thanks, all of you—a good day's work.' He went away, unhurried as usual, to cast an eye on the day's patients.

It was too late to do anything about off duty. Rachel sent the student nurses to their tea, left Norah to clear the theatre after Mr Jolly's list and started on the main theatre with Nurse Saunders. The student nurses, back in half an hour, would finish the clearing and still get off duty and she would stay with Nurse Saunders until the night staff came on. Norah protested at this but, as Rachel pointed out, if Mrs Pepys was going to be off sick, off duty would be chancy; Mrs Short, the second part-time staff nurse, only came in twice a week and was terrified of working with the Professor. 'You take your usual evening,' she told Norah, 'and I'll give myself an extra hour or two when we're slack.'

'You didn't go to dinner,' pointed out Norah.

'Nor I did—I'll have to have a good supper to make up for it. I wasn't going to do anything this evening anyway.' It was just as well that she wouldn't be off duty, she reflected silently, or she might be tempted to phone Melville, and certainly if he had phoned her she would have gone out with him. A kind-hearted girl, she had already forgiven him for his show of temper, and was only too ready to apologise for her own snappy remarks.

If she had secretly hoped that there might be a phone call during the evening, she was to be disappointed. She went off duty just after eight o'clock, ate her supper with those of her friends who had also had an evening duty, and went along to the sitting-room to watch the television and drink tea until bedtime.

She was tired after her long day; she was asleep almost as soon as her head touched the pillow. It was two o'clock in the morning when a touch on the shoulder sent her upright in bed. The night runner was standing beside her bed, holding a mug of tea and looking anxious.

'Sister, I'm sorry but could you come back on duty? There has been a demonstration, I'm not sure where, and we are admitting. The accident room's full and Professor van Teule and Mr Jolly and Mr Reeves are there and quite a few patients need surgery.'

Rachel gulped the tea, wide awake now. 'Get someone to phone Sidney Carter and get Nurse-Walters up, will you please?' It was no use wanting Norah; she lived out, and, besides, if she was going to be up half the night, Norah would have to take the morning's list. Rachel dressed with the speed of long practice, plaited her thick rope of hair into a securely pinned bun, rammed her cap on top and sped silently through the hospital to the theatre wing.

The night runner was there, laying up with the general set, but when she saw Rachel she said breathlessly, 'Oh, Sister, may I go? They're up to their eyes downstairs and Night Sister said if you could spare me . . . '

'Of course. Many thanks for getting started—it's a great help. Ask Night Sister to let me know what's coming up first, will you?'

'A very nasty multiple stab wound,' said the Professor from behind her. 'God knows what we'll find once we start looking. George is setting up a drip but time is of the essence. Where are your nurses?'

'Nurse Walters will be here at any moment and I've asked them to get hold of Sidney.'   'My dear girl, there are a dozen or more in the accident room—we'll need both theatres. I'll be here, Mr Jolly next door and

Mr Sims will use the operating room in the accident room.'

'I'll be here,' said Rachel calmly, 'with Sidney and Nurse Walters, junior night Surgical Sister will be with Mr Jolly and I'm sure that night super will rustle up someone for Mr Sims.' She started to scrub. 'Norah will be on at eight o'clock. If we're not finished she can take over, and there will be two student nurses and the little junior on at half past seven.'

'Nicely organised.' He smiled faintly. 'What a pity you can't organise your own life as efficiently, Rachel.' Before she could do more than open her indignant mouth, he was leaving. 'I'll be up in ten minutes,' he told her over one shoulder.

Nurse Walters came then, pop-eyed with the excitement of being got out of bed in the middle of the night but anxious to play her part. Rachel left her to the manifold tasks around the theatre, and got herself gowned and masked and gloved. She had her trolleys and Mayo table laid up by the time the patient arrived with Dr Carr and a moment later Sidney came quietly in with a laconic, 'Hi, Sister, here's a fine thing. Two o'clock in the morning, too—they ought to know better, getting honest folk out of their beds. What's coming up first?'

Rachel told him as he began to assemble the equipment the Professor might call for, checked her swabs and stood patiently until the Professor with Billy joined them.

'Ready, Sister?' he asked quietly, and then, 'George will come up presently; he's got his hands full downstairs for the moment. The next case is a man with a ruptured kidney.'

He waited while Billy arranged the sterile towels and sheet over the patient and then put out his hand for a scalpel. It was some time later, when he had found and assessed the damage and begun to repair it, that he observed, 'I've asked for some of the day staff to be called on duty at six o'clock—your nurses among them, Sister—no objections?'

'None, sir—thank you for thinking of it.' She passed Billy the intestinal retractor, nodded to Nurse Walters to count swabs, and cast an eye over her trolleys. There was no one to lay up for the next patient, of course; there would be a delay while she cleared theatre with Nurse Walters's help and laid up again. Sidney would help, of course, but they would be a bit pushed. It was almost four o'clock when the Professor took off his gloves and prepared to leave the theatre.

'Finish off, Billy, will you? Sister, I'm going downstairs to see what's happening. Ten minutes?'

She nodded. Nurse Walters was already clearing; Rachel's painstaking instructing was paying off. She helped Billy with the dressings and wheeled her trolleys to one side as the porters came in to take the patient to the intensive care unit. Dr Carr went too and so did Billy, and she and Sidney and Nurse Walters began to clear and presently to lay up once more.

The Professor did a nephrectomy on the next patient since it was hopeless to do anything else. The man was young and looked healthy and there was no reason why he shouldn't make a good recovery.

'Another multiple stab wound coming up,' the Professor told her towards the end of the operation. 'A teenager—he's in a pretty poor state. Can you cope or would you like a rest until the day staff come on?'

'I'm not tired,' said Rachel, uttering the lie loudly to make it sound more convincing. 'Do you want a break, sir?'

'After this next case. George will be up presently and Billy can go down and do some stitching.' He glanced over at the young man. 'You've done very well, Bill—thanks.'

It wasn't possible to see Billy's gratified face, but they could all see the way he flung out his chest. Just like the Professor, thought Rachel, to remember, even when up to his eyebrows in work, to give credit where it was due.

The Professor took infinite pains with the boy; he had been severely wounded and lost a lot of blood, but, as the Professor pointed out to George, the lad was young and although undernourished had a good chance of recovery. 'I shall want him on strict observations, though; see to it, George, will you?' He busied himself with tubing and some meticulous stitching and presently cast down his instruments on to the Mayo table. 'He should do now.'

He glanced at the clock. 'Seven o'clock—we'll break for half an hour, Sister.' He looked around him. 'Ah, reinforcements, I see.'

They had been there for the last hour but he had been too engrossed to notice that. Nurse Walters had slipped away in response to a nod from Rachel and Nurse Saunders had taken her place with Nurse Smithers hovering in the background. Rachel asked, 'What comes up next, sir?'

'An internal haemorrhage, but we don't know why at the moment. Put out everything we've got, will you?' He glanced at her, seeing her tired eyes above the mask. 'But you will have breakfast first, Sister.'

She was only too glad to obey him. Norah, always punctual, had come on duty earlier than usual. Rachel handed over to her with a thankful sigh and went down to the canteen, more than thankful to see that Dolly, appraised of the situation by a friend of hers on night duty, had arrived and gone straight to the theatre kitchen to make tea and cut sandwiches. Rachel told Norah to let each nurse in turn have ten minutes for refreshments and warn Dolly that, once they started again, the surgeons would most certainly need something to keep them going.

The canteen was crowded with night staff eating breakfast, day nurses gobbling down a quick meal before going on duty and a sprinkling of nursing staff who, like Rachel, had been got out of their beds during the night. Rachel sank down beside Lucy and one of the canteen staff brought over a pot of tea. 'And I'll bring you a nice boiled egg and a bit of toast, Sister,' she promised. 'Still busy are you with them poor wounded?' She added with relish, 'They tell me they're swimming in blood downstairs.'

'You shouldn't believe all you hear, Ida,' said Rachel. 'It doesn't say much for the hospital staff, does it? Someone has been pulling your leg.'

Ida looked disappointed, so she added kindly, 'But it's very busy in the accident room and we shall be operating for the rest of the day.'

Ida went to fetch the egg and toast and Rachel gave Lucy a tired grin. 'How are things down below?' she asked.

'Well, not quite as bad as our Ida would wish, but bad enough and you're right, you'll be up to your eyes for hours.'

She was right, of course. Rachel couldn't remember such a day; they worked steadily, stopping briefly for coffee and sandwiches. She lost count of time as the day wore on, concentrating on keeping the theatre going without any hitches. She and Norah took over from each other at intervals so that one scrubbed while the other laid up for the next case and then changed over, and with the three nurses on duty as well as Sidney it was possible to send them off for short spells. But the Professor seemed tireless, going ahead with each case with the relaxed air of a man who had slept well and with nothing of an urgent manner to bother him.

The night staff came on early just as the very last case was being wheeled away and, reinforced by extra nurses, they took over at once. Rachel was loath to leave without clearing the theatres, but the night superintendent made it clear that for once she would be overruled. Norah was sent home, the nurses went eagerly to the supper being kept for them and Rachel went to her office. Even if she didn't stay to see that the theatres were closed she still had the books to do. She sat down and pulled them towards her and began to write in her neat hand. She had a good memory, but tonight she was tired and sat frowning, trying to remember the second case. It alarmed her rather that she hadn't an inkling; what was more, the rest of the cases were getting more vague by the minute. She glanced up wearily as the door opened and Professor van Teule came in. He had said goodnight and thanked them all and gone away half an hour earlier and now she cried, 'Oh, not another case . . . '

He shook his head. 'No. Isn't there anyone else to do that for you?' And when she shook her head, 'I've brought the case sheets along—you can get the names and what was done from them.'

She was so grateful that she could have wept. 'I'll take them back to the wards as soon as I'm finished. Thank you very much, Professor.'

He didn't answer but pulled up the second chair and sat himself down on to its flimsy structure. 'I'll read out the names and details, you do the writing.' He didn't give her time to protest, but began at once so that she had to start writing as fast as she could.

When they had finished he collected the case sheets and stood up. 'Now go and eat your supper and go to bed, Rachel. Are you on duty in the morning?'

She nodded. 'But I'll be fine after I've had a good night's sleep.' She smiled at him faintly, looking very tired. 'I must go and see Night Staff Nurse, then I'll go.'

He opened the door for her and she went along to the theatre with a quiet goodnight. He had worked them all hard all day but he had worked twice as hard himself and he had thanked them and bothered to bring the case sheets. He really was a kind man; she couldn't work for a better one. She conferred with the staff nurse, said goodnight and left the theatre wing.

There was still a good deal of activity in the hospital but she didn't heed the various sounds around her. She wouldn't have supper, she decided as she reached the hall, but would go to bed at once. She was halfway across the wide entrance hall when she saw Melville standing there. She stopped and he came striding towards her, arms outstretched.

'There you are at last. The porter said he thought you would be off duty at any moment—I've only been waiting ten minutes or so. I've a rather special evening planned for us, darling—go and put on something pretty. You can have ten minutes . . . '

She looked at him dully. 'I'm going to bed.'

'Nonsense—bed at nine o'clock in the evening? That's for old folk.'

'I'm tired.' It was too much trouble to explain and surely he must have heard about the rioting and the casualties.

He frowned. 'Well, so am I. I've had a hectic day but I don't moan about it.'

She wasn't listening. 'I'm tired,' she said again, and saw him look over her shoulder, his frown deepening.

The Professor had joined them, his vast person unseen and unheard. He said pleasantly. 'Good evening, Mr Grant. Sister Downing has been working since two o'clock this morning with scarcely a break. She is tired. Bed is the best place for her. Very hard luck on you, Mr Grant, but I'm sure that you understand.'

'An hour or two away from this gloomy place in cheerful company will soon put her on her feet. Rachel?'

She didn't speak; she couldn't be bothered. Besides, the Professor was there, doing the talking for her.

Now he shook his head slowly. 'I'm afraid she's rather past that. She's asleep on her feet. Look for yourself.' There was something in his voice which made Melville study her properly. Her face was as white as her cap and, of course, her dark blue cotton uniform didn't do much for her. Her hair was untidy, too. He said sulkily, 'I can't see what business it is of yours.'

The Professor's voice was genial. 'My dear fellow, Sister Downing is responsible for the management of the theatre wing, its staff, its equipment and so forth.

She assists me and my registrar and the three other consultant surgeons. She needs to be one hundred per cent fit and on her toes. At the moment she is on her knees. If she doesn't get to bed soon she will be flat on her face—something to be avoided at all costs. I'm sure that you will agree with me?'

While he had been speaking he had moved between Rachel and Melville and the latter found himself being edged neatly towards the door which, when he reached it, the Professor politely opened for him. 'I know you will understand.' The voice was still genial but very firm. 'Goodnight, my dear chap.'

He followed Melville outside and stood on the steps watching him get into his car and drive away, and then he went back inside to where Rachel was standing exactly where he had left her.

He put a hand on her arm, nodded to the interested porter in his box, and towed her outside, across the forecourt to where the Rolls was parked. The cool air of the April evening revived her a little, but when she began uncertainly, 'Why . . . ' he hushed her soothingly. 'I'm taking you to have a meal—you won't sleep on an empty stomach.'

'I'd rather go to bed.'

'And so you shall. You shall be back here and in bed by ten o'clock.'

He stuffed her into the car, got in beside her and drove out into the street, and she sat back without arguing. He had said ten o'clock and she knew him well enough to know that he did what he said.

He was driving west through the city, using side streets, and presently she stopped wondering where they were going, noticing only that they had reached quiet streets, lined by town houses of some size. He stopped at length and when he got out and went round and opened her door she got out, too. They were in a narrow street, quiet too, lined by tall narrow houses. It was dusk by now and there were lighted windows and trees at the pavement's edge, so that London seemed very far away even though they were in the heart of it. The Professor took her arm and urged her up shallow steps to a black painted door. There were orange tulips in the window boxes on either side of it and she said, 'Of course, you live here . . . '

'Of course I do'. The door opened and, obedient to his hand, she went inside.

The hall was long and narrow with a staircase at one side and doors to left and right. As they went in, the door behind the staircase opened and a thin elderly man came briskly towards them.

'Ah, Bodkin,' said the Professor, 'I have brought Sister Downing back for supper; she has been on her feet since two o'clock this morning and she's very tired. Could Mrs Bodkin find something light? Soup and an omelette perhaps? As quickly as possible?'

Bodkin inclined his grey head. 'Certainly, sir. Give her ten minutes. If you will go into the drawing room . . . ' He opened a door and Rachel went into the room beyond. A very pleasant room, large and comfortably furnished and softly lighted. She said matter-of-factly, 'If I sit down I'll never get up.'

For answer the Professor pushed her gently into an easy chair and bent down and took her cap off, smoothed her untidy hair back from her forehead and observed, 'That's better. Don't worry, I won't let you go to sleep.' He moved away and came back in a moment with a glass. 'Drink this, it will wake you up just enough for you to enjoy your supper.'

Which it did. Within minutes Bodkin ushered them into a room on the other side of the hall—smaller but just as charmingly furnished as the drawing-room—and this time they had company: a labrador, who came in with Bodkin and the soup, greeted his master, inspected Rachel and went to sit by the log fire while they ate. They talked little as they had their soup, and after the first few spoonfuls Rachel discovered that she was hungry after all, so that she was able to polish off the omelette with a good appetite, and the caramel cream which followed it. She was given lemonade to drink although the Professor had lager, which, he explained, might make her wake up too thoroughly, and presently, when they had finished, Bodkin, who had served them in a fatherly way, asked her if there was anything else she fancied, for Mrs Bodkin would be only too glad to get it for her.

Rachel thanked him and said no, but would he thank Mrs Bodkin for her delicious supper, and when she had done that, the Professor made no attempt to keep her there; she found herself back in the car being driven through the now quiet streets. Once at the hospital he got out again and walked her through the entrance hall to the door leading to the nurses' home.

'You will go straight to bed, Rachel,' he told her. 'There's a list in the morning and I want you on duty.'

She gave him an owl-like look from sleepy eyes. 'I'll be there, sir. And thank you.' It struck her then that he was as tired as she was—his face held lines she had never seen before—and he had never said so. She put out an impulsive hand and touched his sleeve. 'You've been so kind, and you need to go to bed and sleep even more than I do.'

He smiled a little. 'Sound advice, Rachel—I shall take it.' He opened the door and when she went past him she heard the door close again immediately. It seemed a long way to her room but she reached it at last, undressed, washed her face and fell into bed. Lucy, coming in a few minutes later to see if she was back, found her fast asleep, and crept out again.

A night's sleep worked wonders. Rachel ate a good breakfast, discussed yesterday's emergencies and excitements with her friends and went on duty. There was a list, as the Professor had reminded her; not a very heavy one, she remembered thankfully. She went straight to theatre to see how the nurses were getting on, passed the time of day with Sidney and went to her office. Professor van Teule was there, sitting on her desk. He looked up placidly as she went in; he looked very wide awake, extremely elegant and somehow remote. She beamed at him, wished him good morning and, when he made to get up, shook her head and pulled up a second chair to the other side of the desk. 'Are you altering the list, sir?'

'Yes. The cases I should have done yesterday must be done today. I dislike postponing an operation, for the patient's sake; it's no light matter to screw up one's courage to face a certain day and time only to find that it's all for nothing. Can we possibly do the three from yesterday at the end of the list?'

She said, 'Yes, of course, sir,' without hesitating. Everything would have to be rearranged, of course. Normally there were only dentals in the afternoon, but there were only a few cases for that day anyway. She had planned extra off duty for the nurses—Norah could have gone home an hour early and she would have gone off at five o'clock as the second part-time staff nurse would take over. Now she reckoned that theatre would be in use well into the afternoon; Norah would have to stay until five o'clock, and so would Sidney—she would manage with two nurses and let the other two go after second dinner.

'Thrown a spanner in the works, have I?' asked the Professor watching her face.

'Not at all, sir. We're all on duty, it's just a question of rearranging things.'

He finished his writing and closed the folder. 'Your professional calm isn't easily shaken, is it, Rachel? You should learn to apply it to your own life.' And, at her astonished gasp, 'I speak with the best of intentions.'

There was a knock at the door and Norah came in most opportunely, for Rachel couldn't think what to say to that. They plunged at once into ways and means and presently the Professor went away, remarking that he would return at nine o'clock.

The moment the theatre corridor doors closed behind him Rachel burst out, 'Sometimes he is quite impossible!' and, at Norah's surprised look, 'Oh, just something he said; nothing to do with work. Now, which two shall I send off duty this afternoon?'

The day, busy though it was, went smoothly enough; theatre was empty and pristine in its surgical cleanliness by four o'clock. Dentals had been finished long ago and even if Norah hadn't been able to go off duty early at least she had got away punctually, as had the nurses. It only remained for Rachel to clear up her desk, con the next day's lists for Mr Jolly and Mr Sims and check that CSU had sent up a sufficiency of supplies.

Until she began on this comparatively easy task she hadn't spared a thought for anything other than her work, but now her mind, free from the day's urgencies, roamed free once more, and settled, not unnaturally, on Melville.

She couldn't remember very well what she had said on the previous evening; she had been too tired to think clearly or to remember what she had said. She could remember clearly, however, seeing Melville being ushered out of the hospital by the Professor. She hadn't cared two straws about that at the time, but now she winced at the memory. Melville would be annoyed and she excused the annoyance, for no one had made it clear why she was tired. If he had been working all day at the studio, he would most likely have had no knowl-edge of the rioting and the number of casualties. She forgave him without a second thought, never doubting that he had forgiven her once he knew the rights of the case.

The part-time staff nurse came on duty, and Rachel handed over thankfully; an early night, she promised herself, but first she would phone home and, after supper, wash her hair. There were no letters for her but she hadn't expected any; Melville would write or tele-phone when he was free and he would know that she wouldn't want to go out that evening. She had a long satisfying talk with her mother, promised to go home on her next weekend off and went along to the sitting-room to read the papers until it was time to go to supper. Most of her friends were off duty, too, but the talk was desultory. Reaction after yesterday's activity had set in and they sat about, yawning their heads off and scanning the headlines or watching the television. No one wasted much time over supper either; as if by common consent, they all went to their beds. Rachel curled up and, already half asleep, wondered what

Melville was doing. Then rather to her own surprise, she found herself thinking about the Professor. Having an early night, she hoped; he deserved one.

The Professor was doing something quite different, however; he was on a flight to Amsterdam. And as for Melville, fortunately for her peace of mind, she had no means of knowing that he was living it up with one of the actresses working on the current production; a pretty, empty-headed girl, a marvellous companion for an evening's fun. She knew how to dress, too, and there was no fear at all that she would want to leave early.

The next couple of days were uneventful, enlivened only by the arrival of red roses from Melville. The card said all his love, but there was no mention of him seeing her. Too busy, Rachel decided, arranging them in a vase she had borrowed from the private patients' wing. Perhaps at the weekend he would be free, at least; if he phoned she wouldn't go home as she had planned.

The Professor arrived for his usual list in the morning, placid as ever, but with little to say. Only when George asked him if he had had a good time in Holland did he reply briefly that yes, he had. Rachel, pouring their coffee after the list, paused with the jug upheld.

'Oh, is that where you've been?' She frowned. 'But you were here at the beginning of the week.'

He spoke briefly. 'It only takes fifty minutes to fly to Amsterdam.'

Somehow she felt snubbed. She continued her coffee pouring; she wasn't in the least interested in where he had been anyway, and she would take care not to ask questions again. Just occasionally she glimpsed a side to him which wasn't placid at all.

Melville phoned that evening; he was desperate to see her but he had to go to Paris—on location, he explained. He would see her the moment he got back; he longed to see her, he added.

She was disappointed, but his job was important to him; she didn't know much about it, but he wasn't quite his own master. She thanked him for the roses, told him not to work too hard, told him with candour that she longed to see him again, and rang off. She had quite forgotten all the Professor's good advice.

CHAPTER FIVE

RACHEL wasn't unduly worried when she heard nothing from Melville; she had the roses to reassure her and he had told her that he would be away. Besides, she had a lot on her mind. Mr Sims and Mr Jolly both had heavier lists than usual and both theatres were in use. It wasn't until three more days had gone by that she went on duty feeling vaguely worried. Surely Melville would have had time at least to telephone her? She could always ring his office but he disliked her doing that, so even if she knew where he was there wasn't much she could do about it.

It was Professor van Teule's list that morning. It would be a long hard day, for he rarely finished before the early afternoon and although Norah would be there to take dentals, one of the student nurses, Nurse Smithers, a steady, conscientious worker to be relied upon, had days off and Nurse Walters had asked for an evening, which left Rachel with little Saunders. Mrs Crow would be in to take over at five o'clock and the pair of them would manage well enough. Rachel shut the off duty book and looked out of the window. The view wasn't really a view; the forecourt and beyond it the busy street and a vista of small houses and shabby little shops, but it was a May morning, the sky was blue and the sun shone. It was her weekend off—she would go home even if it meant not seeing Melville. The garden would be lovely and she and Mutt would walk miles and come home to one of her mother's splendid teas . . .

'Nothing better to do than daydream?' asked the Professor mildly as he came in. He glanced out of the window in his turn. 'And it has to be daydreaming with a view like this one.'

She turned to wish him good morning. 'I was thinking how nice it will be to go home this weekend.'

He raised his eyebrows. 'What about Melville? Surely he will want you to stay in town?'

'He's—he's away . . . '

'He'll be back,' observed the Professor easily. 'Take him home for the weekend.'

'Oh, well, yes——He might find it a bit quiet . . . '

'Surely not if you are there, Rachel?'

She eyed him thoughtfully. 'You think so? He might have other plans.'

He sauntered to the door. 'Remember what I told you? Stick to it, dear girl. I'll be up in ten minutes or so.'

He didn't refer to their conversation again. For one thing there was little opportunity to talk and for another, although he was his usual placid self, he was remote, so that even if she had had the chance to say anything she would have hesitated to do so.

At the end of the day, with him gone and the theatre once more ready for use at the drop of a hat, she had time to think about his suggestion. Going off duty presently she decided to take his advice, if and when Melville phoned, and if he was reluctant she would go home all the same.

There was a phone call for her while she was at supper and, quite forgetful of the Professor's advice, she tore along to the phone in the nurses' home.

'Melville!' she was breathless with delight. 'I'm so glad you've phoned, it seems ages . . . '

'You've missed me, darling girl?' He sounded pleased, smug almost.

'What shall we do this weekend—I hope you're free?'

'I'm going home.' She said it quickly before she could change her mind. 'Why don't you come too?'

He was silent for so long that she had time to regret her words, then, 'Why not?' I could do with a breath of country air. I'll drive you down, darling—Friday evening—but I'll have to get back on Sunday evening.'

'I'll be ready about six o'clock,' she told him happily, 'and I don't mind coming back early. Have you been very busy?'

'I'm exhausted; you have no idea how hard I work— nose to the grindstone and all that—but it's going to be a smash hit when it's finished.' There was a pause before he said, 'Must go, darling, there's a meeting I have to attend—plans for next week and so on. See you on Friday.'

She went back to her supper, cold on the plate by now. She put it on one side and poured herself a cup of tea. 'You look like a cat that's been at the cream,' observed Lucy, eyeing her across the table.

'I'm going home for the weekend—Melville's driving me down.'

'Oh, very nice. Do I hear wedding bells?'

Rachel went pink. 'Heavens, no. He's up to his eyes in some new production; he never has a moment to himself.'

They left the table together and Rachel went to phone her mother.

Mrs Downing expressed herself delighted to be seeing Melville, concealing her real feelings in a masterly fashion; moreover she assured Rachel that her father would be equally delighted.

'What will I be delighted about?' asked Dr Downing, coming into the room as she put down the receiver.

'Melville is bringing Rachel down for the weekend, dear. I said you'd be delighted to see him.'

'Well, I won't,' declared the doctor vigorously. 'I don't like him and never shall—can't think what Rachel sees in the fellow. Conceited pompous ass.' He sat down at the table to eat a delayed supper. 'Why couldn't she fall in love with a man? That Professor who brought her down a week or two ago—nice chap. Got a wife already, I suppose.'

His wife murmured suitably. The Professor would do very nicely for Rachel, she thought fondly, and she didn't believe that he was married; he had looked at Rachel once or twice . . . 'Oh, well,' she said comfortably, 'things always turn out for the best.'

Her husband grunted; he didn't think that it would be for the best if Rachel married Melville. He was an old-fashioned man; he couldn't think why they weren't engaged if he was so keen on her—she was keen enough on him, more was the pity.

The fine weather held, Friday was a warm day and it was still lovely as Rachel hurried to the hospital entrance just after six o'clock. Melville was there, waiting for her. He didn't get out of the car. 'Hello, darling. Sling your bag in the back and hop in. Do we stop for a meal on the way or have something when we get to your home?'

If she had expected a rather more love-like remark, she suppressed her disappointment. 'Mother will have supper for us,' she told him and was mollified by his kiss. 'What a heavenly evening—I'm so looking forward to the weekend.'

'So am I. Off we go then.'

Too fast as usual, he narrowly escaped the Professor's Rolls as he turned on to the street. Rachel caught sight of the Professor's face as they shot past. He didn't smile; in fact, he looked so stern that she hardly recognised him.

Melville liked to drive fast. Rachel liked to drive fast, too, but she thought privately that sometimes he took risks, overtaking with no regard for oncoming traffic and getting very impatient when he got held up. She wasn't quite as calm as usual by the time they arrived, but the sight of her mother at the open door quietened her frayed nerves. Melville stopped with a flourish and jumped out, opened her door for her and helped her out, keeping a hand on her elbow as they went the short distance to the door.

Clearly calculated to impress me, thought Mrs Downing, and I'm not impressed. But she greeted him charmingly, kissed Rachel warmly and led the way indoors.

Rachel paused in the doorway though and gave a great sniff of delight.

'Can't you smell everything growing?' she demanded happily.

Melville glanced round him; it wasn't quite dark and a faint breeze rustled through the trees behind the house. 'Absolutely heavenly, darling—paradise after town.'

The doctor was in the sitting-room; he kissed his daughter, shook hands with Melville and offered them drinks. Melville embarked on a witty description of his work—he was good at it and they listened with apparent interest, wanting to hear about Rachel's share in the emergency over the rioting. But there was no chance. Melville held the stage and was of no inclination to allow anyone else on it. He had, allowed Mrs Downing, a certain attraction: an amusing way of putting things, a good line in melting looks, too. My poor Rachel, she though, don't let her get too hurt.

Rachel was happy. Melville was at his most amusing; surely her mother and father could see what a successful man he was, and how attractive. She followed her mother to the kitchen presently to help carry in the supper and, once there, 'You didn't mind me bringing Melville, Mother?'

'Not a bit,' said Mrs Downing stoutly. 'It was a very good idea of yours, darling.'

'Actually, it was the Professor who suggested it to me,' said Rachel, incurably honest, so that her mother, who had been harbouring gloomy thoughts, suddenly felt quite cheerful.

'The papers were full of that riot.' She withdrew a steak and kidney pie from the oven. 'Were you very busy, darling? You said very little over the telephone.'

Thinking about it it didn't seem quite real. 'Well, yes, I was, but so was everyone else. I got up at two o'clock and we worked right round until the evening.'

'And then you went to bed, I hope,' prompted her mother.

'Well, no.' Rachel was dishing young carrots. 'Melville came round—he didn't know, you see—but I was too tired to go out. The Professor took me to his house and gave me supper and brought me back to the hospital.'

'How kind.' Her mother bent her head over the potatoes she was mashing. Prayers get answered, she reflected vaguely.

'Supper's ready,' she said aloud. 'Will you fetch the men, darling?'

Melville continued to entertain them during supper, and when Mrs Downing managed to insert some remark about the rioting and the subsequent state of emergency at the hospital, he paused only long enough to say lightly, 'Yes, these demonstrations can be so tiresome, Mrs Downing. It's best to ignore them.'

She was too polite to question that; it was Dr Downing who said gravely, 'That's all very well, but if the hospital staff had ignored the casualties, there would have been several deaths—there were some serious injuries, you know.'

'I'm sure you are right, sir,' agreed Melville. 'What would we do without our ministering angels?'

He smiled with charm at Rachel, who smiled back but couldn't forbear from remarking, 'Well, we wouldn't have been much good without the medical staff.'

'Ah, yes, we must give credit where credit is due, but don't let's get gloomy, darling. You're home now in this lovely old house.' Melville took the conversation into his own hands again and the hospital wasn't mentioned again—at least, not until Rachel and her mother had gone up to bed, leaving the doctor to entertain their guest.

Rachel was brushing her hair when her mother came in, sat herself down on the bed and said, 'Now, darling, I want to hear all about what happened that night, and don't leave anything out . . . '

It was nice to be able to talk about it to someone who listened and was really interested. Rachel started at the beginning and recited the night's events, skating over the bit when Melville had come to take her out for the evening, making the excuse that he had been working all day and hadn't known anything about the rioting. Mrs Downing, who had her own ideas about this, merely said, 'Of course, darling. How kind of the Professor to see that you had a meal and went to bed. You must have been exhausted.'

Rachel put down her hairbrush. 'Yes. I do believe that I was. He's got a charming house in a quiet little street with trees, and a nice man called Bodkin who runs it; his wife does the cooking.'

Her mother bit back the obvious remark that he wasn't married. 'When one has been going full tilt for a long time, it's very nice to have someone there to get one back on one's feet,' she observed. 'Now, jump into bed, love, and have a good sleep. Do you and Melville plan to do anything tomorrow?'

Rachel plumped her pillows into maximum comfort. 'I don't know; he didn't say. I'd like to go for a good walk and take Mutt; I dare say that's what we'll do.'

They went for a walk, but not the kind of walk that Rachel had hoped for. Melville pointed out after a mile or so that he wasn't wearing shoes fit for country lanes. It hadn't rained for several days and Rachel had happily set out along a rutted track, its winter mud turned to a powdery dust, her feet sensibly shod, happily oblivious of Melville's discomfort. She was instantly contrite and led the way back to the road, much to Mutt's annoyance. 'Little Creed is just down the road,' she told Melville. 'It's the prettiest place and we can take the lower road home.'

'Darling girl, what a great healthy creature you are. It sounds lovely but I've just remembered that I promised to phone my producer.' He glanced at his watch. 'Can we get back to your place in twenty minutes or so?' He took her arm and kissed her cheek. 'I'd forgotten all about it but what do you expect when I'm with the most beautiful girl in the world?'

She was far too sensible to believe that, but it sounded delightful all the same. While she whistled to the disgruntled Mutt and turned for home, she thought she would have to get used to Melville's work constantly disrupting his free time, but she quite understood. His was an important job and it had to come first. She left him to his telephoning and went in search of her mother.

'Back so soon?' asked that lady, in the kitchen busy with getting the lunch.

'Well, yes. Melville remembered that he had to phone someone. Shall I make coffee?'

They spent the rest of the day indoors, playing two-handed whist and, after lunch, listening to Melville's amusing conversation. Rachel sat enthralled, taking in every word; it wasn't until she was getting ready for bed that night that she suppressed regret at a wasted day. Well, not wasted, she hastened to correct herself—it could never be that while she was with Melville—only it had been so glorious out and she was able to see so little of the country. Her final waking thought was the hope that he wouldn't mind going to church.

To her surprise he didn't. He had a pleasing tenor voice and sang the hymns with great feeling, listening with great attention to the sermon, his handsome profile uplifted to the pulpit, and when they left the church he took her arm in a protective fashion, smiling at anyone who caught his eye. Her heart swelled with pride as they walked back to the house. Her mother, some way behind with her father, voiced her feelings quite fiercely.

'He is not the right man for her, dear. That was an act in church—all that pious singing and charm. I bet he hasn't been in a church for years. But it was an audience, and he has to have that. My poor Rachel. I can't think what's got into the girl.'

Her husband patted the hand on his arm. 'She's infatuated, my dear, and naturally. She's been working at that hospital for years and the only men she has met have been doctors. Then along comes this Melville with his man-about-town manners and sweeps her off her feet. But it won't last; she's going to come a cropper, poor girl, but she'll be none the worse.'

'That Professor she works for . . . Do you suppose . . . '

'Shall we wait and see, my dear?'

It was a warm, sunny afternoon. Rachel pottered in the garden while Melville lay in a deck chair, his eyes closed. He had a busy week ahead of him, he had assured her, and needed to relax. They went back after tea and as they drove he made various plans for meeting her. No definite dates, he warned her, his work wouldn't permit that, but he hoped that when he did manage to get free she would be free, too.

She would do her best, she told him earnestly, remembering uneasily that Norah had a week's holiday and that neither Mrs Pepys nor Mrs Crow could be expected to cover for her at a moment's notice.

'A lovely weekend.' he told her when they arrived at the hospital. 'I enjoyed every moment of it,darling. Life is so empty when you aren't with me.' He kissed her.

'Now I must dash—I've work to catch up on.'

She remembered uneasily what the woman at the party had said and dismissed the thought as disloyal. 'When shall I see you?' she asked.

'As I said, darling, I can't say at the moment. But the minute I'm free I'll give you a ring.' He drove off and she picked up her bag and went through the hospital, back to her room, to phone her mother and then to gather in Lucy's room with such of her friends as were off duty and to drink tea. She had no reason to feel depressed, she told herself; it had been a marvellous weekend and Melville had been simply great. Perhaps it was because they had to meet at odd moments whenever he was free, and so often, when he was, she wasn't. If only they could spend more weekends at her home. But the disquieting thought that he might be bored refused to go away; he was a man who liked living in London; he liked parties and theatres and crowds of people, and she supposed that given time, she would get to like them too. Just at the moment, though, she was homesick for her parents and Mutt and the peace of the country. Bed would be the best place and a good night's sleep.

But she slept badly, waking often with a vague worry at the back of her mind. It was a relief to get up and somehow comforting to eat breakfast in the company of her friends, talking shop, the outside world for the moment forgotten. It was equally comforting to find the Professor sitting at her desk, studying a pile of Path Lab forms. His 'good morning' was friendly and his casual enquiry as to whether she had enjoyed her days off uttered in such a placid tone that she heard herself saying, 'Not very. At least, the weather was heavenly and it was so nice to be at home . . . It was a bit quiet for Melville . . . '

'With you there?' He sounded surprised. He aban-doned the Path Lab forms and sat back looking at her. 'I have a very strong feeling that you ignored my advice; you probably agreed to every word he uttered and sat about doing nothing much while all the time you were longing to stretch your legs.'

'Well, yes. You see, he hadn't got the right shoes to go walking . . . '

The Professor allowed a small sound to escape his lips. 'Ah, that of course might make things difficult.' He examined his beautifully kept nails. 'You will not of course take my advice—why should you? But refuse his next invitation, Rachel.'

'Why? He asks me out because he—he likes me to be with him.'

'That is why.' He got up, sweeping the papers before him into a neat heap. 'I shall be in X-Ray if anyone wants me. We start at nine o'clock, do we not?'

He was gone with a careless nod.

His list was fairly straightforward which, seeing that Norah wasn't there, was a mercy. Nor did he waste much time over his coffee once they were finished, only discussed the cases with George, thanked her with his usual politeness, and wandered away to look at his more recent cases on the surgical wards. Rachel sent Mrs Pepys, who had just come on duty, to her dinner with two of the student nurses, and cleared the theatre with Nurse Saunders's help. George had a couple of minor operations for the afternoon and Mrs Pepys could scrub for them while Rachel got on with the books and forms. When that lady came back from her meal, Rachel went down to the canteen to eat roast lamb and two vegetables and treacle tart for afters. For some reason she had lost her appetite, and her friends sitting with her made sure they lost no opportunity to make pointed remarks about being in love. They teased her gently and didn't believe her when she said that she didn't know when she and Melville would be going out again.

After the ordered urgency of the morning's list, the afternoon seemed dull. She did her books, carried on mild arguments with the CSU and the pharmacy, and a more heated one with the laundry, saw Mrs Pepys off duty and went into the theatre to check any instruments which might need repair. Mrs Crow, coming on duty at five o'clock, sent her thankfully off duty in her turn,   o have a late tea in the sisters' sitting-room, and then sit around, gossiping until it was time for supper. A dull evening, she reflected, yawning her head off as she got ready for bed. An evening without Melville . . . It would have been lovely to go out. Never mind what the Professor said; if he phoned and asked her out, she would go. She lay in bed, deciding what she would wear.

Mrs Crow preferred to have an evening duty, so Rachel was free after five o'clock for the rest of the week, but it wasn't until three days had passed that Melville phoned. He had tickets for a concert, he told her, and how about coming?

Any faint remnants of the Professor's advice flew from her head. Of course, she would love to go; she bubbled over with eagerness and Melville laughed in her ear. 'My goodness, what's come over you, darling? You're usually tied up and here you are bursting with enthusiasm. I'm flattered.'

A tiny doubt had crept into the back of her mind; had she been too eager? But it was too late now; she agreed to be ready by seven o'clock that evening and to meet him in the entrance hall. 'And what shall I wear?' she asked anxiously.

'Oh, something pretty. We'll have a drink first; the concert doesn't start until half past eight.'

'What sort of concert?'

'Oh, a bit highbrow, darling, but everyone who's anyone will be there.'

She wore a silk jersey dress she hoped he didn't remember and arrived at the front door exactly on time—a mistake, because Melville wasn't there. But Professor van Teule was, strolling in, presumably to cast an eye over his patients. She stood there and he stopped when he saw her and shook his head.

'Oh dear, oh dear. I fear you have cast wisdom to the winds again, Rachel. A quiet dinner or is it dancing?'

She caught the amused gleam in his eye and frowned. 'We're going to a concert and really, Professor van Teule, you have no right to question what I do in my free time.'

He didn't answer her, only smiled gently. 'Take-in from midnight, isn't it? But of course you will be back in the hospital by then, and here is, er, Melville.'

Melville's 'darling' was a bit too fervent but Rachel didn't mind; it would give the Professor something to think about. He said so little, she thought worriedly, and yet he disquieted her. She wished him goodnight in a cold voice and smiled brilliantly at Melville, quite certain that the evening was going to be marvellous.

They went to a small bar in Soho and she enjoyed every minute of it, even though Melville remembered the dress, adding kindly, 'But of course it was too short notice for you to pop out and get something new.'

One day, she resolved firmly, she would explain to him that she simply couldn't buy a new dress every time she went out with him. Luckily he forgot it very quickly, plunging into an amusing anecdote about a well-known film star whom he had met that very morning.

The concert was well patronised; the hall was filled with fashionably clad women and men smoking cigars. They had seats in the stalls and Melville didn't hurry to reach them, stopping to greet people as they went. And once they had settled down, he spent the time pointing out the various famous people around them. 'I may have to leave you now and again, darling,' he told her and squeezed her hand. 'Must show my face, you know.'

The orchestra filed in and presently began to play. Rachel liked music, with a bias towards Rachmaninov's concertos and Debussy, Chopin and Grieg, but she was quite unable to understand the weird sounds coming from the orchestra. 'Brilliant composer,' whispered Melville. 'Modern music is the only thing worth listening to. He's all the rage.'

Rachel could hardly bear it. To take her mind off the strange sounds she began to work out the off duty for the next fortnight in her head, and, that done to her satisfaction, did a mental check of the extra instruments the Professor would need in the morning, which led to wondering what he was doing at that moment. Whenever she met him off duty he was either going to or coming from the surgical wards or theatre. Surely he must enjoy some leisure? And he had vaguely mentioned that he hoped to marry . . . His fiancée must be a long suffering girl. And a lucky girl; the thought had flown into her head quite unbidden.

Melville left her during the first interval. 'I shan't be a moment, darling,' he explained. 'There are one or two people I must speak to. I'll bring you a drink.'

She sat, feeling lonely, until the lights dimmed and he reappeared, to catch her hand in his. 'Darling, I'm so sorry—I couldn't get away. Have you been very lonely without me? We'll go to the bar after this next concerto, I promise you.'

The thought of a drink sustained her through the next half-hour of weird sounds and when the lights went up at last she followed him to the bar, already packed with people.

They found a corner and he went in search of drinks, to come back presently with two glasses. 'Martini, darling,' he told her and she felt a little prickle of irritation that he hadn't asked her what she wanted; she loathed Martini.

He had taken barely two sips when he exclaimed, 'Good heavens! There's Guy. I simply must have a word with him.' And he had gone again, disappearing into the dense crowd around them. She put her untouched drink down on a convenient ledge and looked around her. Women in ultra-fashionable dresses hemmed her in, escorted by men who, unlike Melville, didn't keep dashing off to see someone or other. She couldn't see him anywhere, and presently she edged her way out of the bar and went back to her seat, feeling hard done by. The evening, from her point of view, wasn't being a success; the music was frightful and she might just as well have been on her own. Which wasn't quite true but she was in no mood for niceties.

When Melville rejoined her she said coldly, 'Guy must have had a lot to say.'

'Darling, you're cross.' He took her hand in his. 'And I'm grovelling, really I am. We'll have supper somewhere to make up for it. I'm truly sorry; do forgive me.'

And of course she forgave him. She loved him, or she thought that she did. They sat through the last excruciating medley of sound and then, with only the minimum of pauses while Melville greeted the people he knew, they got into the car and drove to the Ivy Restaurant. It was full of well-known faces, Melville told her gleefully, and presently there would be even more. 'And choose what you like, my angel, I can put it on the expense account.'

A remark which upset her. Would he have taken her to this expensive place if he had had to pay for it out of his own pocket? It was a question which bothered her throughout the meal so that she was rather quiet.

'A bit out of your depth?' asked Melville kindly. 'Rubbing shoulders with the famous is a bit awe-inspiring until you get to know them, as I do.'

She swallowed an oyster patty, not liking it over-much. 'Do you really? Know all of them?' It was difficult not to be impressed, although she had no wish to meet any of them. 'Do you enjoy meeting them?' she asked.

'My dear girl, of course I do. Success—successful people—they matter.'

She wasn't sure what prompted her to say, 'And people like Professor van Teule, who is very successful as a surgeon, although he never appears in public . . . '

Melville laughed. 'You don't quite follow me, darling. I'm talking about the success which brings you before the public eye. I dare say your Professor is clever enough in his way, but who wants to know about his work? I mean, it's something one doesn't talk about, isn't it?'

Which, she had to admit, was true.

He took her back to the hospital soon afterwards, kissed her fervently, assured her that he would see her soon, and drove off. She got ready for bed slowly, mulling over her evening. The music had been awful and it had been a pity that Melville had had to spend so much time with his friends and leave her alone, but he had been an attentive and amusing companion and she was quite sure that she loved him to distraction.

'A pleasant evening, I hope?' enquired the Professor suavely as he went to scrub before his list. 'Where was the concert?'

She told him briefly and he said, 'Ah, that new conductor—all the fashion at the moment, I believe. Modern music, was it?'

'Very,' said Rachel and went back to her trolleys, subduing a strong desire to tell him just how awful she had found it. He would have listened and, even if he was a devotee of the stuff, he would have given her his full attention.

The list was an exacting one. The Professor, as he always did, carried on a desultory conversation with his companions, touching on a variety of subjects, but music wasn't mentioned, nor did he refer to it while they had their coffee break. When at length he had finished, he bade them all good day, added his thanks, and went unhurriedly away. For some reason Rachel felt frustrated; she had prepared herself for his observation about her evening, and steeled herself against the advice he gave so readily. It was a bit of a let down.

At dinner Lucy warned her that there was a badly injured child in. 'Fell off a high wall, face downwards. Professor van Teule has had a look and he wants to operate; he was talking to George when I came to dinner. You'll get the good news when you get back.'

He was waiting for her, standing with his back to the office, looking at the chimney pots. He turned round when she went in.

'There's a child for a splenectomy. Can you be ready in twenty minutes or so?'

'Certainly, sir. Boy or girl?'

'A little boy—ten years old—fooling around on a demolished block of flats.'

'Oh, the poor lamb. Is his mother with him?'

'No, she hasn't been traced. There doesn't seem to be a father.'

'Someone must look after him—love him.'

'They're looking for his granny; she works somewhere in the Mile End Road.'

'Doesn't it make you furious?' She had gone to stand by him, sharing the deplorable view. 'Can you keep him as long as possible?'

'Yes. He can go to the country branch when he's fit again and we must see what we can do about Granny. A temporary job close by, perhaps?'

'The world's a funny place.' Rachel was voicing her thoughts, hardly aware that she was sharing them with him. 'All these dressed-up people yesterday evening, listening to that frightful music, and being what they call successful. They're not, you know; they don't do anything that matters.' She gave a great sigh. 'You do.'

She didn't see his slow smile and the gleam in his eyes.

'Thank you, Rachel. But it takes all sorts to make a world. I take it that you didn't altogether enjoy your evening?'

'The thing is,' she told him seriously, 'Melville is so popular. When we go out he meets so many friends he has to stop and talk to.'

'But you must meet a number of famous people?'

'No,' she said slowly. 'You see, he thinks—quite rightly—that I wouldn't have much in common with them.'

'I feel sure that he is right.' He glanced down at her and walked to the door. 'You're off duty at five o'clock?'

She was already unpinning her cap. 'Yes, sir.' She followed him out and went to theatre to make sure that it was ready for use; the nurses had done very well. With that she went to scrub and presently, standing by her trolleys, she watched him, gowned and masked, join those waiting for him round the table. He asked, 'Ready, Sister?' in his unhurried voice and she handed him a scalpel, reflecting how nice he was to work for.

CHAPTER SIX

THE splenectomy was followed by a baby girl who had swallowed an open safety pin. The Professor extricated it, his large strong hands as delicate as thistledown, and then went away to reassure the anxious mother. He was back again before Rachel had the theatre just so once more.

'Mr Jolly is taking over until tomorrow morning. Billy will assist him if anything comes in. I'm going over to Welbeck Street.' He had private patients there. 'George and his wife are coming to dinner; I wondered if you would care to join us? I haven't asked you earlier because I wasn't sure if you had a date.' He added, 'You know Rosie?'

Rosie was George's wife of less than a year, a nurse like herself who had been working at another London hospital. Rachel had met her and liked her and an evening out would be nice . . . Melville had said that he was going to be very busy; it was unlikely that he would want to take her out. She said, 'Thank you, Professor, I should like to come.'

'Good—nice for Rosie to have another girl to chat to. I'll be outside at seven o'clock.'

He had gone his unhurried way before she could reply.

There was time to shower and change at her leisure and spend time on deciding what she should wear. It had been a warm sunny day but now that it was early evening, it had turned a little chilly. She decided on a patterned Italian jersey dress which she had worn only once because Melville had declared it to be totally without eye-catching appeal. She had pointed out at the time that she had no wish to catch eyes anyway, but all the same she hadn't worn it again. It was a pretty dress though, in shades of soft pink with a high neck and long sleeves. She put on a light coat, patted her hair into final tidiness and went down to the entrance. As she went she reflected that she could have kept the Professor waiting for ten minutes—after all, he was always advising her not to be too eager—but somehow she didn't want to do that. For one thing he wasn't Melville . . . She wondered about the girl he was going to marry—in Holland, presumably, or she would have been at the dinner party and she herself would not have been invited.

The Professor was leaning up against the Rolls's bonnet, talking to Mr Jolly, but he straightened up when he saw her and the two men walked towards her, greeted her pleasantly, passed the time of day for a few moments and then parted, Mr Jolly to go into the hospital and they to get into the car.

'George and Rosie will join us just before eight o'clock.' He started the car and slid out into the street. 'You look nice.' He sounded just like one of her brothers and she felt instantly at ease.

'Thank you. What a lovely evening, even in London.'

'You like the country, don't you, Rachel?'

'Yes—oh, yes. I was born and brought up in Wherwell, and of course the hospital is in the wrong end of London, isn't it?'

'Where it does the most good.' They were nearing his home and she thought it wasn't so bad for him, living in a pleasant street with trees and probably a garden behind the house. In fact, she decided, one could live quite happily in such surroundings, with the park not too far away and the sound of traffic nicely muted.

Bodkin had the door open before they had crossed the pavement and bade her a dignified good evening before closing the door after them and throwing open the drawing-room door. The Professor urged her in, saying to Bodkin over his shoulder, 'Mr and Mrs Cook will be here in a few minutes, Bodkin. Show them straight in, will you?'

There was a log fire in the steel fireplace but the french window at the end of the room was open. 'Come and see the garden,' he invited.

It was larger than she expected, with a little fountain at the end of a stone path and trees all round so that the houses on either side were quite hidden. There were flower beds on either side, crammed with wallflowers and late tulips, and at the end there were roses. Not yet in flower, but she guessed that in a few weeks' time they would be magnificent.

They strolled to the end and back with Toby trotting beside them.

'It's beautiful,' she sighed, 'to come back here after a hard day's work. Do you like gardening?'

'Yes, when I can spare the time. A gardener comes and does most of the work, though.' He looked towards the house. 'Here are George and Rosie.'

The evening was delightful. Not a celebrity in sight, thought Rachel naughtily, and instantly felt disloyal to Melville, but it was so nice to sit quietly knowing that when her companions looked at her it was with detached friendliness and not with the sharp eyes of critics.

No one mentioned hospitals or patients during dinner. The conversation was light-hearted and the food delicious and afterwards, when they had had coffee, the men strolled into the garden, and Rachel and Rosie sat gossiping gently, clothes and holiday plans and the exciting news that Rosie and George were expecting a baby. 'Not until November,' said Rosie. 'I wish I could knit.'

'I can—let me know what you want. It will make a nice change from the sweaters I wade through for my brothers. Does Professor van Teule know?'

'Yes, George told him the moment we were certain. He is a dear, isn't he?'

Rachel said slowly. 'Yes, he is. He is always there.' An obscure remark which Rosie immediately understood.

'I haven't mentioned your Melville—I wasn't sure if you'd mind, but everyone knows about him at the hospital. He's very glamorous, so I'm told. Is he great fun? You must meet masses of famous people.'

'Well, I've seen them, but I haven't met them— Melville says I'd find it difficult to talk to them. I mean, I don't know a thing about the stage and TV and all that, and they certainly wouldn't want to know about hospitals.'

Rosie made a sympathetic noise. 'When we married I thought, oh, good, no more hospitals. I can be a married lady and keep house and have time to read the paper. Well, it's not like that at all. George comes home and gives me a blow-by-blow account of some super operation Professor van Teule has done; I don't know why I don't wear uniform . . . '

Rachel laughed. 'You know you wouldn't like anything else and it must be super for George to go home and talk to someone who knows what he's talking about.'

Rosie giggled. 'Yes, I suppose you are right. Professor van Teule must feel awfully lonely sometimes; I mean, no one to unburden himself to. He goes out a good deal—lots of friends—but that's not quite the same thing, is it?'

Rachel agreed that it wasn't, but before they could pursue this interesting topic further the two men joined them and they sat and talked for an hour until George declared that they must go home.

Rachel got up to go too and George said at once, 'We'll give you a lift, Rachel.'

'I'll drive Rachel back,' observed the Professor, at his most placid. Rachel knew from long experience of working for him in theatre that the more placid he was the more determined he was to have his own way. She made no demur for it would have been of no use; besides, she enjoyed his company.

Perhaps rather more than he enjoyed hers, she wondered, when, the moment George had left, he urged her, in the nicest possible way, to get into his own car. It was a depressing thought, but she kept up a cheerful flow of small talk until they reached the hospital, where she prepared to alight without waste of time. The Professor's hand clamped down on hers on the door handle. He said to her surprise, 'I wonder why it is that I am able to know what you are thinking despite the social chatter? And no, I am not anxious to be rid of you; at least not for the reasons you are mulling over.'

He bent his head and kissed her cheek gently. 'Stay there,' he bade her, and got out to open her door and walk her to the hospital entrance.

'I have no idea what you're talking about,' said Rachel in a chilly voice.

'Of course you haven't. Later on, perhaps . . . Good night, Rachel. It was a delightful evening; thank you.'

She gave a gurgle of laughter. 'You've said my lines. It's me who's thanking you, Professor.'

'What deplorable grammar. Perhaps we both enjoyed ourselves equally.'

'Well, I do hope so. I loved every minute of it and thank you very much.' She added ingenuously, 'You see, the food was delicious and I didn't have to worry about what I was wearing . . . ' She stopped and went very pink. 'Oh, I do beg your pardon. That sounds awful, but it wasn't meant to be. What I meant was, I felt quite at home. You see, I'm not much good at parties.'

She stopped because she could see that she amused him; he must think her very silly and gauche. Apparently he didn't. 'You are a nice girl,' he told her as he opened to door. 'Don't try and change, Rachel.'

She went past him and the door swung to. As she crossed the entrance hall she couldn't resist looking to see if there was a letter or a message for her. There wasn't.

It was four days before she heard from Melville again. A note, dashed off in a hurry; he had been so busy, too busy even to phone her, but he couldn't wait to see her again; he would take her out to dinner that evening and call for her at eight o'clock.

She wondered what she would have done if she hadn't been off duty that evening, but as it was, she was free; the day suddenly became wonderful, her eyes shone with delight, she was bubbling over. The Professor, coming to collect some of his instruments to take with him to the nursing home where he was operating, paused to look at her. After a moment he observed, 'Melville is taking you out; am I right?'

'Yes, Professor. How did you know?' She smiled widely; she couldn't help herself.

He said rather shortly, 'You look happy. I wonder if Melville knows what a lucky man he is . . . '

She blushed. 'Oh, thank you, but that's not quite true. You see, you only know the sensible side of me, the theatre sister; but me, out of uniform, I'm not sensible at all—or perhaps I'm too sensible, I'm not sure; I think that sometimes I fall very short of Melville's standards.'

The Professor picked up the bundle of instruments she had ready for him, shook his head at her and walked away without a word. An unsatisfactory end to their rather strange conversation. She put it out of her head, though, and fell to thinking about what she would wear that evening.

Not the blue; Melville had said that it didn't suit her. She decided on a pale patterned silk dress, sleeveless and plainly cut. It had been an off-the-peg bargain, chosen for its unassuming good cut, soft colours and excellent fit, Moreover she knew that it suited her and it did a lot for her. She went off duty punctually and spent a long time getting ready. She was pleased with the result and, unheeding of the Professor's advice not to be eager, hurried down to the entrance at exactly eight o'clock. Excitement and happiness had rendered her positively beautiful and Melville, sitting behind the wheel of his car, kissed her with a most satisfactory warmth.

'Darling, how I've missed you and how beautiful you look. We are going to have a wonderful evening. The Savoy, no less, and we'll dance the night away.'

He began to tell her about his work, making her laugh a great deal; she hadn't felt as happy as this for a long time. The happiness was only a little marred as they entered the foyer of the restaurant. Melville, waiting for her while she went to hand in her wrap, watched her coming towards him under the bright lights of the chandeliers.

'That's quite a nice dress,' he told her, 'but, darling, can't you be a bit more—well, eye-catching? You've got a splendid figure but you don't show it. Now if you went to one of the good dress houses they would do you proud.'

She refused to be put out. 'Don't be absurd, Melville, I can't afford those kind of clothes. If you don't approve of what I'm wearing then I'll go back to the hospital.'

He caught her arm, laughing. 'Oh, darling, you look lovely in rags, I'm sure, and now I've got you here at last, I'm certainly not letting you go again. It's only that I want you to look more beautiful than any other girl around.' He gave her a long look. 'You are that already.'

Very extravagant talk, thought Rachel with her usual good sense, instantly swallowed up in delight; the evening was going to be sheer heaven and Melville was the most marvellous man in the world.

Marvellous he was, too, ordering dinner and champagne and dancing with a careless grace, murmuring in her ear, holding her hand across the table. But it was unfortunate that as they danced he should see friends, who came back to their table with them and were presently joined by two more. They introduced themselves by first names, were carelessly polite to her and then, when the talk centred around the studios and their work, inevitable she was forgotten. Even when someone did ask her opinion of some actor or actress or some TV show, she was forced to admit that she didn't know much about those things, so that they looked at her in astonishment. It was obvious to her that any way of life outside their own was of no interest to them at all. She smiled and smiled until her face felt as though it would crack and felt relief when someone suggested that she should dance again.

She found herself partnered by a cheerful young man who danced well and hadn't much to say—or perhaps, she thought guiltily, he thinks I'm too stupid to talk to. But she enjoyed dancing with him and presently she danced with Melville who held her too tightly and murmured in her ear, 'So sorry about this, darling, but you see how it is. They're a jolly lot really.'

She agreed cheerfully. 'They must be nice to work with,' she observed.

'Lord, yes. A damned sight nicer than that lethargic fellow you work for. I can't think how you stick it, Rachel, working in that dreary hospital day after day.'

She didn't answer because he never listened to her when she tried to explain that she loved her work and that the Professor wasn't in the least lethargic. They finished the dance and went back to their table and found the other four on the point of going. 'Promised to pop in on Tommy's party,' said one of them. 'See you around, Melville.' They smiled at Rachel—they had already forgotten her name, but she had forgotten theirs, too.

It wasn't very late. All the same, Melville said as they sat down, 'I expect you want to get back, darling. Shall we go?'

A little disappointing, really. She had hoped that they would have stayed for another hour and danced, but it was thoughtful of Melville to see that she got back in good time. She fetched her wrap and got into the car beside him. It was a warm night, starlit and with a bright moon, and London streets were fairly empty, offering a spurious charm. Rachel had a sudden urgent longing to be at home in the garden, sweet smelling and quiet . . .

'That was a piece of luck meeting that lot,' said Melville. 'They're marvellous company—never a dull moment when they're around. You were a bit quiet, darling.'

'Well, I haven't seen any of the shows they were talking about or the people in them . . . '

'Which bears out what I'm always telling you. You should go out more, enjoy life, meet people instead of spending your days and half your nights in that gruesome place. Look, my sweet, give up this job of yours; no one will miss you. I can get you into some show or other; you're pretty enough and with a decent wardrobe you would make the grade.'

'Grade to what?'

'Why success, of course; fame, darling, money, the bright lights.'

She said patiently, 'But Melville, I don't want any of those things. Can't you understand that I'm happy as I am?'

They were in sight of the hospital and its ugly bulk against the night sky put her in mind of the Professor and his advice.

To her own great surprise, she said strongly, 'If you don't like me as I am, then we'll stop seeing each other, Melville.' He had stopped before the door and she got out quickly. 'Thank you for a delightful evening and my dinner.'

She marched away, her head in the air, taking no notice of Melville's angry astonishment, although the temptation to look round was very great. She stalked through the entrance hall to find a group of men in the middle of it. Too late, she remembered that the hospital consultant staff were to have met the hospital management committee that evening. The meeting was over, but a large handful of learned gentlemen had paused to chat on the way home.

They paused in their talk as she went towards them and eyed her with appreciation. Her colour was high, her eyes sparkled, she looked ready to do battle and, if they had but known it, she was ready to burst into floods of tears, too.

She circled the group with a vague, glittering smile, not really seeing any of them. It was the Professor's long arm which gently brought her to a halt. 'Ah, Sister Downing, the very person I wished to see. I was on the point of leaving you a note . . . '

He excused himself to his companions and said blandly, 'If you will come a little on one side—I shall take up only a few minutes of your time.'

She had no choice. They stood a little apart and he leaned his length against a marble column bearing the bust of the hospital's founder.

'Norah's back?' he asked, and, when she nodded, 'Good. There's not much doing in the morning, is there? The theatre sister at the nursing home has been taken ill and there is a gastroenterostomy which needs to be done. If I pick you up at eight o'clock tomorrow morning, will you take the case for me? I'll arrange things at the office.'

She stared up at him, her head still full of her quarrel with Melville, and he said quietly, 'You're upset.' He took her arm and walked her away to the back of the entrance hall where the centre lights hardly penetrated.

She said woodenly, 'I told him I wouldn't see him again. He wants me to leave here, and I won't. He doesn't understand. I—I said, I . . . ' She gulped. 'I took your advice, for what it's worth.' She looked at him miserably. 'I don't know what I'm going to do.'

The Professor smiled. 'You're going to bed and to sleep and then in the morning you will take my case for me, and I am willing to bet my fees against your salary that there will be roses or a phone call or a letter by tomorrow evening. You see,' he added gently, 'I know a good deal more about men that you do, Rachel.'

He gave her a gentle shove. 'Off to bed with you and don't dare cry.'

He opened the door to the nurses' home for her, wished her a quiet goodnight and went back to his companions. And as for Rachel, she went to her room, undressed, crying her eyes out as she did so, and then tumbled into bed and went to sleep at once.

There was a message for her at breakfast; would she hand over the theatre keys to her staff nurse and accompany Professor van Teule, not forgetting to notify the office upon her return? There was no time to brood over Melville. She explained to Norah, gave her the keys and hurried down to the entrance. The Rolls was there with the Professor at the wheel, reading *The Times*. He opened the door for her, folded the paper, wished her a placid good morning and drove without further ado to the nursing home.

Really it was a private hospital, Rachel decided as she got out before its imposing entrance. 'Do you do a lot of surgery here?' she asked as they crossed the splendid hall.

'Oh, yes. Did you sleep?'

'Yes, thank you. You have a very busy life.'

They got into the lift and he pressed the button for the third floor. 'And a lonely one.'

'But not for long. When you're married . . . '

'You believe that to be the answer?'

'Well, of course. You'll go home to a wife who loves you and I expect you'll have lots of children and you'll never be lonely again.' The lift stopped. 'I didn't know that you were lonely. You must have heaps of friends.'

'Oh, I have. One cannot marry friends.'

He led the way down a wide corridor and through swing doors. 'Here we are, and here is Staff Nurse White who will show you where everything is.' He gave her a reassuring smile. 'I'll be along in ten minutes or so.'

Staff Nurse White was young and pretty and pleased to see her. 'Gosh, Sister, I'd have died if the Professor had told me to scrub. I can manage an appendix or tonsils or something easy but I've only been here a week or two. I'll show you round.'

The theatre was all that could be desired. Rachel poked her nose into cupboards and shelves, made sure

she knew where most things were, and went away to
scrub and lay up. There would be another nurse beside
Staff Nurse White, and Dr Carr would be anaesthetising. There was a resident house surgeon who would
assist the Professor.

There were no problems; Dr Carr greeted her as
though he had expected her to be there anyway, the
house surgeon was a serious young man and the second
nurse seemed sensible. The operation was a lengthy
one, but once it was over, Rachel was borne away to
have coffee with Staff Nurse White. The Professor had
gone, presumably to see his patient in ICU and she
wondered if she should make her own arrangements to
return to the hospital. But there was no need for that;
he came back presently, asked her if she was ready and
accompanied her to the car.

'I could have gone back on my own,' she pointed out.

'So you could. There is the devil of a lot of traffic
around; you might have got back by tea time. Thanks
for your help, Rachel.'

'I enjoyed it.' And she had. It had prevented her from
thinking about herself and Melville; she would have
leisure enough in which to do that later on. The
Professor hardly spoke on the way back. He had a
teaching round that afternoon; perhaps he was
thinking about that, thought Rachel, and, after a few
attempts at small talk, she fell silent.

It was during the afternoon that the flowers arrived,
an extravagant bouquet with a card attached. From
Melville, just as the Professor had said. She put them
in the washbasin in the cloakroom and tucked the card
in her pocket, its message already learned by heart.
'Forgive me, darling, I am broken-hearted'.

She was clearing her desk just before going off duty when the Professor poked his head round the door. 'Any flowers yet?' he wanted to know. She paused in her writing.

'Yes, and a card.' She couldn't stop the wide smile.

'Good. You have, of course, forgiven him; he only has to phone and you will rush to meet him where and when he tells you to. Don't, Rachel. Wash your hair or whatever you do in the evenings; have a headache if you prefer something more romantic. Go home for the weekend. He'll still be here when you get back.'

'You're very severe. Just supposing he thinks I don't want to see him again?' She gave him a sharp look. 'Professor, you don't approve of me and Melville—it seems to me that you're discouraging him.'

He came round the door and sat on the side of the desk. 'My dear Rachel, why should I do that? I, who am to be happily married as soon as it can be arranged. My sole object is for you to be happy, because happy people work well. And I like my theatre well run.' He stared down at his beautifully polished shoes. 'You are an excellent theatre sister.'

For some reason this civil comment annoyed her. She would have liked him to have thought of her in a different light, although she was very vague as to exactly what. She thanked him frostily and turned her attention rather pointedly to her books.

The Professor got off the desk and wandered to the door. 'I'm going up to Edinburgh tomorrow,' he told her casually. 'I'll see you on Monday.'

He strolled away with a cheerful nod and presently she finished what she was doing, fetched her flowers, and went off duty, feeling peevish. She put this unusual feeling down to the fact that she wasn't spending the evening with Melville. She missed him, she told herself, arranging her bouquet in a large jug she had purloined from the downstairs pantry in the nurses' home.

Which made it all the more strange that when Melville rang her the following morning she firmly refused to make any arrangements for the weekend. 'I promised to go home,' he was told firmly. 'My brothers will be there and we don't see each other all that often.'

'Am I not to be invited?' he asked sulkily.

She almost weakened. 'Well, there wouldn't be any room for you . . .'

There would have been, if he were the kind of man one could ask to double up with one of her brothers, but he wasn't and regrettably she was sure that none of her brothers would be prepared to give up a bed for him. They didn't know him well and she was honest enough to admit that they had very little in common with him. She said placatingly, 'I do usually get a weekend each fortnight, Melville, and I'll have days off some time next week.'

'Oh, well, I suppose I'll have to exist without you then.' He sounded mollified and she took advantage of it.

'I miss you, too,' she told him.

'I'll give you a ring after the weekend,' he said, and his goodbye was abrupt enough to worry her.

The weekend came and with it a phone call from Norah's eldest child to say that Norah was in bed with a heavy cold—perhaps 'flu.' It was too late to get either Mrs Pepys—who wouldn't have come anyway—or Mrs Crow. Rachel phoned her mother and resigned herself to a weekend on duty.

Saturday was quiet—an emergency appendix which George dealt with, a teenager with superficial stab

wounds and an elderly woman with a severed artery in
her upper arm. Sunday was even quieter; it wasn't take-
in, so that road accidents and the like went to another
hospital and the minor surgery could be done in the
accident room. Rachel sent Nurse Walters off duty,
handed over to a staff nurse borrowed from the accident room, and went off duty herself.

The fine evening stretched before her, a waste of
several hours which she didn't intend to spend indoors.
She could phone Melville, of course . . . He had said
he would ring her after the weekend, but that was
because he had thought she would be at home. She
showered and changed while the idea of going to his
flat and giving him a lovely surprise took shape in her
head. The more she thought about it, the better it
seemed.

It would mean a long bus ride but it was still early
evening. She hurried through the hospital and crossed
the courtyard to the street beyond and the bus stop,
and the Professor, on the point of turning into the
hospital yard, saw her and frowned thoughtfully. She
should be at home; he had been pretty sure that she
would take his advice, so what had happened to make
her change her plans?

George enlightened him. 'She told me she'd be off
duty at five o'clock—I dare say she's going to meet that
fellow who's always sending her flowers.'

The Professor said carelessly, 'Probably,' and began
to talk about his list in the morning. He had a nasty
feeling that Rachel was in for an unpleasant surprise
but there wasn't much that he could do about it.

Rachel sat in the almost empty bus, thinking about
Melville and how pleased he would be to see her. She
had never been to his flat, but she knew where it was.

She was walking down the elegant street where he lived when she saw him. He was mounting the steps to the front door of the flats where he lived, his arm flung carelessly round the shoulders of a willowy girl. Blonde, as dainty as a fairytale princess and dressed in the forefront of fashion. Rachel's eyes didn't miss a single detail; they didn't miss the way he bent and kissed the girl as they reached the door, either.

She was quite close to them by now, but they didn't see her. They went inside the elegant entrance and she stood looking at the empty doorway, not seeing it at all. Presently she turned on her heel and started walking back the way she had come. She walked quite a long way before she realised that she was tired, and got on a bus. She walked into the hospital as the Professor, apparently on his way out, crossed her path.

He took a quick look at her white, stricken face and observed cheerfully, 'Hello. Back early, aren't you? Did you have nice weekend?'

She was tired and very unhappy but she did her best to answer him.

'I didn't go home—Norah isn't well so I took her duty.' To her mortification her eyes filled with tears. 'I went to see Melville; he was with a girl . . . such a pretty girl, too.'

She tried to pass him but the Professor was a bulky man, not easily circumvented. Besides, the hand he put out, though gentle, was firm.

'A strong drink will help.' He turned her round and marched her out of the hospital again. 'I know the very place; you shall tell me all about it while you have it.'

'I don't want . . . ' began Rachel and didn't bother to go on. The rest of the evening had to be got through and the Professor's impersonal concern made him an easy man to talk to, and if she didn't talk to someone she would have hysterics. She had never had them in her life, but she felt sure that they must be a great relief. To lie on the ground and kick one's heels in the air and scream held a distinct appeal.

She got meekly into the car when he held the door open, reflecting that it was getting to be quite a habit; it was nothing short of a miracle that he should appear, large, placid and comforting. She was behaving badly, like a teenager in the throes of first love; he might find her an excellent theatre sister, but she was deplorably lacking when it came to managing her own life.

She sat silent while he drove, so busy with her thoughts that she hardly noticed where they were going: Duke's Hotel, in a quiet cul-de-sac near St James's Park.

She was swept inside the restaurant. 'I'm hungry,' declared the Professor. 'We might eat something.'

It didn't enter her poor worried head that he might have gone home to the meal which Mrs Bodkin would undoubtedly have ready for him. She sat down at a secluded table and obediently sipped the sherry he ordered for her.

When the menu cards were brought, he ordered for her: cold cucumber soup, omelette Arnold Bennett and a water ice. Having done that, he embarked on a conversation about nothing at all, allowing her time to pull herself together.

By the time they had finished their meal, she was feeling much better, sufficiently herself to tell him what had happened. In the telling, she did discover that it wasn't as bad as she had imagined it to be. Bad enough, but there were so many reasons why Melville was with the girl; it was harder to think of reasons why he had been kissing her with such satisfaction, but, as the Professor reminded her, people in show business treated kisses and endearments in a different light to the man in the street.

'What shall I do?' It was the kind of question she might have asked her eldest brother.

'Nothing, and if you have the will-power to be unavailable for the next week, be that, too.' He sighed. 'I've told you that already . . . '

'Yes, I know. You're very kind to help me, Professor. And I really will take your advice this time. Only when he's waiting for me and I see him I—I find it very difficult to be unavailable.'

He looked thoughtful. 'You need to put a few hundred miles between you.' Just for the moment the heavy lids flew open, revealing blue eyes with a decided gleam in them, but she didn't see that; she was looking down at her coffee cup. When she looked up at him again, she saw his usual placid face. 'I feel much much better, thank you.'

'Good. I'll take you back.' Which he did, bidding her a pleasant goodnight when they reached the hospital. She went to bed at once and slept soundly, rather to her surprise.

Norah was back on duty in the morning. Rachel heaved a sigh of relief at the sight of her; there was a heavy list and after midnight they would be on take-in again. She inspected the theatre, allotted jobs to the nurses, left Norah to lay up for the first case, and went to the office. There were the usual forms to deal with and she meant to get them done before the Professor arrived, for once work started she had little chance of getting back to her desk.

She had picked up the first form when the office rang for her to go there at once. She banged the receiver back into its cradle, cross that she was to be interrupted, warned Norah, and went down to the ground floor to see the principal nursing officer.

Miss Marks was middle-aged, imposing and distant in her manner. No one liked her overmuch, although everyone admitted that she was fair, an excellent organiser and a splendid disciplinarian. Rachel stood quietly in front of her desk and waited to hear why she was there.

She was surprised to be told to sit down; relieved, too—it couldn't be anything too awful. What was more, Miss Marks smiled thinly at her.

'I have had a letter, Sister Downing, which I think will be of great interest to you. There is to be an international conference of theatre sisters, to be held in Basle, and you have been nominated to represent our group of hospitals. It is in eight days' time and will last for one week, during which time you will attend lectures, visit hospitals and attend discussions. I will see that you get the details later. You will of course be granted special leave for this.'

Typically she didn't ask if Rachel liked the idea. She bowed her head majestically, said, 'Thank you, Sister, that will be all,' and opened a file of papers before her.

'Do I have to go, Miss Marks?'

Miss Marks looked annoyed. 'Of course, Sister. This is an honour both for you and for the hospital.'

There was no more to be said. Rachel went back to the office and found the Professor there, whistling through his teeth and staring out of the window.

His good morning was casual but his glance was sharp. Rachel took off her cuffs and started to roll up

her sleeves. 'Good morning, Professor. Something's
come up. I've just been to the office. Miss Marks tells
me that I'm to go to a theatre sisters' conference at
Basle, next week some time. It seems I have no choice
in the matter.' She paused. 'I suppose I do have to go?'

'Well, this certainly is a surprise,' lied the Professor
smoothly. 'Presumably you will have to go if you've
been nominated. I take it you will be representing the
hospital group?'

She nodded. 'Yes, but is it so important? I mean
there will be hundreds of us there—am I supposed to
pick up useful tips, or something?'

He laughed. 'Well, if you do, don't rush to try them
out on me. How long will you be gone?'

'A week. Not take-in, thank heaven. Oughtn't you
to have been consulted first, Professor?'

'As it happens, Miss Marks has asked if I could see
her later on today. I dare say she thought that you
should be told as soon as possible; she would be fairly
sure that I can have no objection to you going.'

He strolled to the door. 'The first case may present
complications. Put out my own forceps and the special
retractors, will you? I'll be back in fifteen minutes or
so.'

Left to herself, Rachel made no effort to tackle the
forms. The Professor didn't seem to mind her going
and for some reason that upset her, but hard on that
thought came another one: Melville. Even if he wanted
to see her it would be impossible; besides, she wouldn't
be tempted to answer his letter if he wrote, and when
she got back again, who knew? Anything could have
happened. She was a little vague as to what exactly
could happen, but it involved Melville begging abject
forgiveness, sending her armfuls of flowers and having

a perfectly valid reason for kissing that girl.

Considerably cheered by these naïve speculations, Rachel went along to the theatre to tell Norah the news.

CHAPTER SEVEN

EVEN if Melville had got in touch with her—and he hadn't—she would have had precious little time to spend with him. She had a passport but the details of her flight had to be arranged. She was to travel on Monday morning and she would be met at the airport and taken to the Hilton Hotel where the conference would be held. For some reason the programme of the week's events had not been sent but, as her friends were quick to point out, what did that matter? She would be staying in great comfort at an hotel which, according to the brochure, was within a few minutes of the shopping centre, she would doubtless meet a great many people and have a marvellous time and never mind the lectures or discussions. Miss Marks had told her that there would be three other theatre sisters from Great Britain attending, but she wasn't likely to meet them until she got there, for they were from Scotland and the north of England and would fly from different airports.

Busy as she was in her off-duty time, deciding what clothes to take, how much money she would need and the best way to get to Heathrow, she was even busier in theatre, for the Professor's lists were longer than ever and the off-duty rota had to be adjusted to fit in with her absence.

She had rung her mother with the news and, since she was due a weekend anyway, arranged to drive herself home on Friday evening. There had been no letter from Melville and she had thrust him to the back of her mind; time enough to think about him when she got back. Just for the moment there was far too much on her mind.

The Professor showed little interest in her trip. Beyond cautioning her to attend all the lectures and see all she could of any hospitals she might go to, he hadn't much to say. Indeed, he was rather more silent than he usually was and certainly, in his placid way, more demanding in his work. Perhaps he had quarrelled with the girl he was to marry . . .

His list on Friday stretched well into the afternoon, so that by the time theatre was cleared and cleaned and she had handed over to Norah, it was getting on for six o'clock. But it was a splendid evening and driving would be a pleasure after a week of hard work. She hurried to change and get into the Fiat, puzzling over the Professor's decidedly casual manner as he had left the theatre. Perhaps he was sickening for something. On second thoughts, a ludicrous idea, and why was she fussing so? He had been kind and helpful and she liked him but their friendship was impersonal and revolved round their work.

She started the car and plunged into the evening rush hour.

It was late by the time she got home; getting out of London had taken longer than usual and the traffic on the motorway had been heavy. But there was supper for her and her mother and father were delighted to see her, with Mutt barking his head off at the sight of her. She ate her supper while they discussed her trip to Basle and since she didn't mention Melville no one else did either.

'I dare say the surgeons will miss you,' essayed her mother casually.

'Oh, I don't think so. Norah's there for the big lists and the part-time staff nurse can cope with the small stuff. I've not had time to think about it much, I've been too busy, but I think it's going to be fun.'

'How many will there be?' asked her father.

'I don't know. It's an international affair, so there should be quite a few. I haven't got the programme of events—Miss Marks said I should get it when I et there. There'll be lectures and discussions and demonstrations and visits to hospitals . . . '

'And enough time for you to look around, I hope,' observed her mother.

It was lovely peaceful two days, pottering in the garden, driving her father on his rounds, taking Mutt for long walks and sitting in the garden, and in the evenings sitting doing nothing with Everett on her lap. She left after tea on Sunday with the promise that she would telephone when she arrived in Basle, and drove back to the hospital to pack the carefully chosen wardrobe, check her tickets and money, wash her hair and go to bed after a good gossip over mugs of tea with half a dozen nurses crammed into one room.

Rachel had decided to drive herself to Heathrow and leave her car in the garage there. She left after breakfast, speeded on her way by those of her friends who were free to wave her away, and watched by Professor van Teule from the windows of Women's Surgical. The ward sister, flustered at his early arrival, was thrown into a still more nervous state when he bade her a polite good morning and left the ward as suddenly as he had arrived. As she had a lot on her mind it didn't occur to her that her ward overlooked the forecourt and the parking space reserved for nursing staff. And as for suspecting his interest in Rachel, she never gave it a thought; everyone knew that she was head over heels in love with Melville Grant. As for Professor van Teule, she, like everyone else on the nursing staff, liked him, stood a little in awe of him and had no interest in his private life, for the simple reason that he had never given them cause to do so.

It was at the end of the morning's list when the Professor told Norah that he would be away for a week. 'Mr Jolly will deal with anything George considers necessary. Otherwise George will go ahead with Thursday's list—all straightforward cases.'

Norah took the news calmly. 'What a good thing that you and Rachel are away at the same time,' she remarked. 'She won't be back until Monday afternoon. Will you have a list on Monday morning, sir?'

'No. I will not be back until Monday evening or Tuesday morning. George will arrange a list for Tuesday.' He gave her a kindly smile. 'You've enough staff?'

Norah said that yes, she had. Such a nice man; he and Rachel would suit each other down to the ground. She sighed, but here was Rachel hopelessly infatuated with this man Grant, and the professor, from all accounts, about to get married.

Rachel parked the car, took herself and her case through the customs and in due course settled herself in the plane. She didn't care for flying but since she had to do so there was no point in getting worked up about it. She ate the odds and ends on the plastic tray she was handed and took out the booklet on Basle which she had unearthed in a bookshop. It seemed a nice city; she only hoped that she would see something of it.

The airport, after the complexity of Heathrow, was a pleasant surprise. It took no time at all to go through customs and walk outside into the warmth of an early summer's afternoon. She had been told that she would be met and she saw a man bearing a board with her name on it almost immediately. He addressed her in French, to her relief, for she had an adequate smattering of that language, but almost no knowledge of German, and he spoke no English.

The six miles to the city were accomplished in an incredibly short space of time. Rachel, a bit shaken, got out at the hotel entrance, tipped the man and went into the foyer. There were a few people standing about, and at the end of the reception counter was a large board with 'International Theatre Sisters' Convention' written on it. The girl sitting beside the board seemed to know all about her; her name was ticked off on a list, she was given a key to a room on the sixth floor, her bag was handed to a porter, and she was whisked into a lift. All very efficient, but she had no idea what she was supposed to do next. She followed the porter to her room and, when he had gone, inspected it slowly. It was comfortable and the bathroom was more than adequate. There were television and radio, several magazines and a really splendid view from the window. She washed and tied back her hair, then unpacked and, dying for a cup of tea, took herself back to the lifts and down to the foyer.

A large arrow pointed to the coffee shop and she followed its direction briskly. She would have to get a programme and any information there was later but tea was more important.

The coffee shop was pleasant and not too crowded. She drank three cups of tea, ate a mountainous cream cake, and went back to the reception desk.

There was to be an inaugural get-together that evening, she was told, to be held in the reception room on the floor below. When she enquired as to the morrow's timetable, she was told that the day's time-table would be available at breakfast. 'For the first day will be undemanding,' said the clerk. 'The first lecture begins after lunch; you will have the morning in which to integrate. After today, the following day's programme will be given to you each evening.'

There were any number of people in the foyer now, but whether any of them were nurses like herself she was unable to decide. Of one thing she was certain, there wasn't much English being spoken—lots of American accents, French and German, and several languages which might have been from any country. She bought a paper at the hotel shop and went back to her room to phone her mother and then sit down and read the day's news.

The get-together was to be informal, she had been told, and she spent some time debating what she should wear. She decided on an Italian silk jersey dress in various shades of amber, spent an hour lying in the bath and doing her face and hair and, a little after seven o'clock, made her way back to the foyer.

A wide curving staircase led down to the floor below and women of every age, shape and size were going down it. No English, she thought unhappily, exchanging smiles with a stout young woman who addressed her in German and with a delicate little creature, half her size and enchantingly pretty. Rachel, whose ideas about the orient were vague, put her down as someone from the Far East; she looked far too fragile to be a theatre sister.

A get-together wasn't quite the right word for it, she decided after a few minutes. Everyone there was willing and anxious to be friendly but there should have been someone there to start the ball rolling. It was like a gigantic cocktail party, where no one knew anyone else. And what was the point of it all if they were to be lectured in English when, as far as she could make out, almost everyone there was speaking in their own tongue? She took a second drink from the tray being carried around and addressed the two young woman nearest her. They were from Denmark and told her so in an English as good as her own, so that she exclaimed happily, 'Oh, I was beginning to think that nobody spoke English . . . '

They laughed kindly. 'We all speak and understand English but of course we prefer to speak our own language. Are there no other English nurses here?'

'Oh yes. Three I've been told of, perhaps more, only I haven't met them yet.'

'You should ask. I expect they will tell you at the reception desk what their room numbers are and their names. We always do that.'

She hadn't thought of that; obviously she was talking to old hands at the game of nurses' conventions. It was like being a new girl at school. The drinks were loosening tongues and creating a friendly atmosphere. Several more women joined them, two of them considerably older, the other two French and voluble talkers. Presently they drifted to the long table at the end of the room where the food had been set out. Rachel, quite hungry, tucked into cold chicken and salad and listened to her companions' talk. The two

older women were from Austria and had little to say
for themselves although they were friendly enough; the
talk was carried along on the shoulder of the French
girls, who lapsed into their own language most of the
time but contrived to be very amusing all the same.

Rachel, anxious to find the English girls if they were
there, drifted to and fro without success although she
met a nurse from Texas and another from Toronto. It
was an opportunity to find out more about the week
ahead of them but neither girl knew much more than
she did, and anyway, as the American pointed out, they
would be told in the morning. 'And I dare say it will
be a round of lectures and demonstrations and
inspecting instruments and how to deal with student
nurses.'

At about ten o'clock they began to drift back
upstairs and to their rooms. Most of them had arrived
that day and were tired; those who weren't went along
to the bar or the coffee shop. Rachel refused several
invitations to have coffee and went to her room. Her
last sleepy thought was to wonder if the Professor had
had a heavy list. Of Melville she didn't think at all.

She woke early to a lovely day and, since breakfast
could be had in the coffee shop from six o'clock
onwards, she got up, did her face and hair with more
care than usual, got into a sleeveless cotton dress and
went along to the lifts. There didn't seem to be anyone
around, but it was still early and they had been told
that they would have the morning free.

She got out of the lift in the foyer and the first person
she saw was Professor van Teule, elegant in summer
suiting, not a hair out of place and looking, if that were
possible, more placid than ever.

He came to meet her. 'There you are,' he said carelessly, just as though they had arranged to meet. 'I thought you might be up early.'

She goggled at him, her pretty mouth slightly open. 'However did you get here?' she asked, and then frowned because it was a silly question.

'On an evening flight.' He smiled slowly and she said sharply, 'You're one of the lecturers—why didn't you tell me?'

'I had the ridiculous idea that if I had done so you would have decided not to come.' He didn't say why, nor did he give her the chance to answer. 'Shall we have breakfast?'

When they were seated in the coffee shop he said, 'I hope you aren't too annoyed that I am here—I only lecture in the afternoons and there will be no need for you to attend.'

'Well, of course I shall come.' She met his eye across the table. 'And I'm not a bit annoyed; in fact, I'm glad. I know I shan't see you except on the platform but I'll know you are here. I feel like a new girl at school.'

The waitress came with coffee and a basket of rolls and Rachel ordered scrambled eggs. The Professor asked for bacon, eggs, sausages and mushrooms.

'I haven't had a programme of events yet,' said Rachel, pouring coffee. 'We're to get it this morning and the first lecture is this afternoon.'

For answer the Professor pulled a folder from a pocket. 'Normally they chalk the events up on a board each morning—I daresay they'll do the same here. But cast your eye over this if you like.'

The first lecture was at two o'clock in one of the smaller conference rooms. And the Professor was giving it. There would be a discussion afterwards, a pause for tea and then a film depicting new theatre techniques. Those attending the conference would be expected to make notes and there would be a room put at their disposal for this purpose. Dinner would be at seven o'clock and afterwards there would be a lecture on modern methods of anaesthesia. Quite a busy day, and, casting her eyes rapidly over the rest of the programme, she could see that all the other days would be busy, too; lectures either in the morning and afternoon and the evening free, or the mornings free and the rest of the day taken up with various studies. Two trips to hospitals, she was glad to see, and since her flight home didn't leave until around lunchtime she would have several hoursleisure on the last day.

She heard the Professor observe, 'You must see as much of the city as possible while you're here. I'm at the Basle Hotel. I'll give you a ring each morning before eight o'clock and we'll arrange to meet.'

Rachel eyed him thoughtfully. 'That's very kind of you, Professor, but just because you are lecturing here doesn't mean—that you—you have to entertain me.' She took a deep breath. 'Besides, there are three other English girls here—I haven't met them yet . . . '

'Don't try to give me the brush-off, Rachel.' He sounded amused and she went pink. 'The three ladies you refer to are very senior members of their profession. I doubt if you would have anything in common save an exchange of views concerning the running of the operating theatre.'

'Isn't that why I'm here?' asked Rachel with a snap.

'My dear girl, of course, but it wouldn't be much use for you to glean information from those who, like yourself, have come to be apprised of modern methods.' He passed his cup for more coffee, his voice as bland as his face.

'I shall phone you each morning,' he observed in the placid voice which she had learnt concealed a steely determination to have his own way.

She said meekly, 'Very well, Professor.'

He went on calmly, 'The evening lecture will finish about nine o'clock; Dr Geller wants to meet his wife who is flying in on an evening plane from Vienna. I'll wait in the foyer for you; we'll go somewhere and have a drink and you can give me your impression of the day's events.'

She agreed readily. Truth to tell, it would be nice to have something to look forward to at the end of the day, and someone she could talk to freely.

The coffee shop was filling up now. The Professor put down his cup and glanced at his watch. 'I've a meeting in half an hour. I'll see you this evening.' He bade her a casual goodbye and wandered away.

She waited for a few minutes. She didn't want him to think that she was anxious for his company, although it would have been rather nice, she thought wistfully, to have explored a little with him. On her way out she met the three nurses from home. The Professor had been right; they were all on the wrong side of forty, probably first-class theatre sisters but slightly intimidating in appearance. One of them stopped Rachel as she passed them.

'You're Sister Downing,' she observed. 'You're very young—which hospital are you from?'

Rachel said, 'Hello,' and smiled, for, despite appearances, they might be rather nice—one never knew. She named her hospital and the youngest of the three said, 'You must be very proud of yourself—you must be very good at your job,' and returned her smile.

'I dare say we're all much of a muchness. It's a splendid chance to be here and get up-to-date, though.'

'I doubt if we'll learn anything new,' said the woman who had stopped her. 'And I don't care for this hotel; it's far too crowded and noisy.'

It seemed a good idea not to answer that. Instead Rachel said, 'I'm going for a walk, it's such a lovely day. I expect I'll see you this evening.'

'Oh, yes we should keep together—there are a great many foreigners.'

Another remark best left unanswered. 'I won't keep you from your breakfast,' said Rachel and made her escape.

She enjoyed her morning. It was a pleasant five minutes' walk to the main shopping street and she spent an hour looking in windows looking for small presents to take home. Everything was expensive and she hadn't brought a great deal of money with her. Chocolates were the obvious choice, and something special for her mother. She strolled back presently, enjoying the sunshine and the strangeness of it all, stopping to study the price list in the window of an elegant tea-room. The cakes looked mouthwatering but after some mental arithmetic she decided that it was wildly expensive. Perhaps her last day she would go there as a farewell treat.

The foyer of the hotel was full of people arriving and departing; there were piles of luggage around and porters darting about, and the hubbub was considerable. Rachel went up to her room, tidied herself and went down again to look for lunch.

It was in the same room where they had gathered the evening before, another buffet, and, with an appetite sharpened by her walk, Rachel filled a plate with salad and cold meat and looked for a table. The Canadian nurse she had met already was sitting at a small corner table and she beckoned Rachel over. 'Sadie will be here in a minute.' Sadie, Rachel guessed, would be the American. 'Have you been out?'

They exchangéd views of the city, the hotel and the cost of everything and presently when Sadie joined them, began, inevitably, to discuss their jobs. But not too seriously; they laughed a good deal and her three colleagues from home, sitting close by, sent disapproving looks towards their table.

They all had their day's programme by now and began to drift into one of the conference rooms where the lectures were to be held. It was like being back at training school, thought Rachel, sitting with her two companions well to the back. It occurred to her that she had never heard the Professor give a lecture—this one was to be on organ transplants and was going to last an hour with questions afterwards. No power on earth, she told herself, would make her ask a question.

He was introduced by a Swiss Professor of Surgery and he came on to the small stage looking completely at ease and elegant. The Canadian girl dug her elbow into Rachel and hissed, 'I say, he's just not true—look at him. Every girl's dream, I'd say. Am I glad I came.' And Sadie on the other side whispered, 'What wouldn't I give for a chance to get to know him.' She glanced at her programme. 'Dutch, Professor of Surgery in Leiden and London.' She glanced at Rachel, sitting poker-faced between them. 'Have you seen him before, Rachel?'

'Well, yes, he does work in London.'

It was a good thing that there was no more chance to ask questions. He began his lecture. It was a learned lecture, well thought out and delivered with assurance, but Rachel doubted if many of the women there were concentrating on it; the Professor, she had to admit, was quite something. She studied him carefully, and rather to her surprise realised that she had never really looked at him before.

There was an avalanche of questions when he had finished. Rachel, making herself small between her two companions, kept quiet. Any questions she might have could wait until she got back to London.

He went at last after a protracted period of questions and answers and they all went back downstairs again for tea. She was unfortunate enough to bump into the women from home as she stood, teacup in hand, cake balanced on a plate, looking for a seat. They had enjoyed the lecture, they told her; indeed they had all asked a great number of questions afterwards and found the Professor most helpful. 'He would be a pleasure to work for,' observed one of them. 'If possible it would be interesting to meet any theatre staff who have had that privilege.'

Rachel agreed demurely.

It wasn't worth going out again before dinner; Rachel went to her room, lay in the bath for a long time reading an English newspaper and got into a white crêpe blouse and a rose-patterned skirt before going down to her dinner. This time they were seated at long tables for soup, rather small portions of fish with boiled potatoes and no vegetables, and vanilla ice-cream with coffee after. Rachel's shapely person rose from the table, still hungry.

The evening lecture was interesting and ended just as the Professor had indicated, sharp at nine o'clock. There was a general exodus to the coffee shop and the bar, but Rachel went to the foyer. She saw the Professor at once, sitting in a deep easy chair; he looked thoroughly at ease, as though he were on holiday, and for no reason at all she was glad that she was wearing something that she knew suited her.

He came to meet her, smiling pleasantly. 'You look nice,' he told her. 'I've been sitting here watching a succession of stunning outfits going to and fro, and I mean stunning in the correct sense of the word. You're very restful on the eye, Rachel. Was it a good lecture?'

'Yes, I enjoyed it. I enjoyed yours, too.' She was puzzled to feel shy with him, a quite new feeling. Perhaps it was because they were away from their familiar background.

'Thank you. I was pleased at the number of questions at the end of it.' She saw that he had no idea that the questions were asked by an audience who, almost to a girl, would have liked the chance to get to know him. He must know that he was the answer to a girl's prayer, but she doubted if he ever thought about it. There were a lot of people in the foyer by now; some of them had been in the audience recently and they were frankly staring.

'Are you hungry?' asked the Professor. 'I do hope so, I'm famished—I went to a drinks party, for my sins, and there were bits and pieces on little plates—not at all satisfying.'

She laughed and he took her arm as they went out of the hotel. 'There's a charming little restaurant not too far away . . . ' He nodded to the doorman to get him a taxi. 'What have you got on the agenda tomorrow?'

'Instruments in the morning, open heart surgery in the afternoon . . . '

'Evening free?'

'Yes.'

'Good. I'll get hold of a car and we'll see something of the country.' They got into the taxi and Rachel said, 'That would be lovely, but you must have other things you'd like to do.'

'Not on my own. We are two foreigners here; we should join forces.'

He told the driver where to go and sat back beside her.

It was still quite light and there were a lot of people about. Somewhere between the hotel and Marktplatz they took a turning off Freiestrasse and stopped in front of a small restaurant and went inside. The Professor had booked a table, tucked away in a windowed corner of the crowded room, and they sat, talking little, sipping their drinks and deciding what to eat. The restaurant was French, and Rachel opted for lobster Cardinal and a salad while the professor chose sole Colbert and salade Niçoise.

The food was delicious. Rachel popped the last morsel of lobster into her mouth and said, 'What a heavenly meal. However shall I be able to face fish fingers and chips when I get back?'

'Don't think about it. Let us make hay while the sun shines and dine here each evening.'

She blushed. 'Oh, I didn't mean that—that is, I wasn't fishing for another meal, I really wasn't.'

'My dear Rachel, surely we know each other well enough not to consider anything so absurd.'

Which, when she thought about it, made good sense. 'Well, it would be nice to discuss the day's work. Have we been a good audience? I haven't met very many of the other girls yet, but those I have are very keen.'

'Dedicated theatre sisters? It makes a nice change from theatre, though.'

She answered him seriously. 'Well, yes, and some of them have come a long way.' She passed him his coffee cup. 'You're lecturing each day, aren't you?'

He nodded. 'And don't forget the visits to the hospitals. I won't be there, but I know them both; I'm sure you'll find them interesting.'

He went on to talk about Basle after that, and presently, when she said that she should be going back to the hotel, he made no demur but paid the bill and took her back by taxi, wishing her a friendly goodnight in the foyer and waiting there until she had got into a lift.

It had been a delightful evening, she thought sleepily, getting ready for bed. She went to sleep at once without a single thought of Melville.

She was wakened by the phone ringing at half past seven.

'Good morning, Rachel.' The Professor's voice was quiet in her ear. 'I'll be in the foyer this evening—the lecture should be over by half-past seven.' And when she said, 'Yes, all right,' he went on, 'Tomorrow you're free in the morning. I shall be round after breakfast so don't go out.' She said, 'Very well,' because it seemed the natural thing to say, and before he rang off he said, 'I've got a car for this evening. Bring a jacket or something with you, it might get chilly.'

She gave her full attention to the lectures during the day, taking notes and discussing them during the breaks. There were quite a few instruments for her to

follow up, although she doubted if the hospital
committee would stand the expense of getting them.
And the open heart surgery had been interesting
although she hadn't learnt anything new from it; the
Professor had been using the techniques talked about
for some time.

His own lecture was at half-past six. Peritonitis and
how to deal with it. She sat quietly, listening to his calm
voice, and found the hour too short. There was a buzz
of talk when he had gone and she sat for a moment
listening to her companions on either side of her. 'I
wonder where he goes?' Sadie wanted to know. 'Do
you suppose he's married? Perhaps he's got his wife
here—if she is, I wouldn't let him out of my sight if I
were her.' She got up and Rachel with her. 'Ah, well,
let's see what's for dinner. I shan't bother to change
this evening.'

Rachel escaped without appearing to do so. The
Professor had said that he would wait for her in the
foyer and she simply had to change into another dress.
She had brought a stone-coloured jersey dress with a
matching jacket with her; she got into it, did her face,
tidied her hair and shot down to the foyer.

There weren't many people there; it was getting on
for eight o'clock and dinner was in full swing. They
went out to the car he had hired and he drove away
without delay. They went out of the city through the
tree-lined streets and Rachel asked where they were
going.

'We'll cross the river and drive to Freiburg—it's on
the edge of the Black Forest and the scenery is rather
special. There's a good restaurant in a village just
beyond; we'll have a meal there. I think you'll like it.'

'I'm sure I shall. It's such a heavenly evening, too—
it's nice to be out of doors. Have you had a busy day,
Professor?'

'My name's Radmer . . . '

'Oh, is it? It's Dutch, of course.'

'Certainly not—it's a Friese name. My home is in
Friesland; I was born there. We are as touchy about
being called Dutchmen as a Scotsman would be if one
called him an Englishman, and yet we are united with
the rest of Holland, just as Scotland is to England.'

'You don't mind living in England?'

'No, I've made it my second home for a number of
years and I can go to Friesland easily enough.'

'But when you marry—you said you were going to—
will you stay in England?'

'Yes, for the foreseeable future.'

They had left the last houses behind and he went on,
'I'm going to take an inner road. It will take a little
longer but it is much quieter.'

A hint nicely put for her to mind her own business.
She said brightly, 'That sounds nice,' and fell to
thinking about Melville. If he had been beside her
instead of the Professor he would have been telling her
outrageous stories about the famous people he rubbed
shoulders with—he could be an amusing companion.
The Professor wasn't amusing, although he had a sense
of humour. He was restful, she decided and returned
to her thoughts of Melville. He might not like so much
peace and quiet—the road ran through wooded
country with here and there a glimpse of a castle
crowning a hill, and infrequent villages tucked cosily
around steepled churches. She said, speaking her
thoughts out loud without meaning to, 'I don't think
Melville would like this,' and she felt awful the minute

she had said it. 'I don't know why I said that . . . '

'Because he is on your mind—at the back of your head, whatever else you are thinking or saying.' The Professor sounded matter-of-fact and not in the least put out. 'I think you must miss him: the excitement of being taken to dinner at fashionable restaurants, meeting show people, finding flowers waiting for you when you go on duty, living on the heights and then plummeting down to the depths. Have you told him where you are?'

She didn't pause to think how strange it was that she could confide so easily in her companion. 'No, I took your advice and made myself unavailable. It worked before.'

'And will again.' His voice was kind. 'We are almost at Freiburg. We shall not stop there but go on to the restaurant; it's just this side of Emmendingen.'

He knew the area fairly well, he told her, but didn't enlarge on that, only pointed out the minster as they drove through Freiburg and shortly afterwards stopped at a restaurant tucked in among the trees well away from the road.

The restaurant was a charming place and well patronised. Rachel, feeling adventurous, chose sweet wine soup, river trout from the Black Forest with a lettuce and bean salad, and finished with savarin with strawberries and whipped cream.

They ate leisurely, enjoying the warm, light evening and talking comfortably about nothing in particular, drinking the rather dry wine the Professor had ordered and then when they had finished, lingering over their coffee.

'I wouldn't want to live here, but it would be a heavenly place to stay for a while.'

The Professor passed his cup. 'A honeymoon, perhaps? You said that Melville might not like so much peace and quiet, but Basle isn't far away, you know, and Strasbourg is almost as close. There's plenty of night life in both places if one is so inclined.'

'I hadn't thought about—about honeymoons,' said Rachel, who had thought of very little else for weeks— ever since she had met Melville. And then, at his look, she blushed. 'Well, yes, I have, but there's nothing definite . . . He's so busy, you see, Professor.'

'Radmer. Of course.' His voice was dry.

He drove her back along the road bordering the Rhine and crossed the river by the Dreirosenbrucke, through the outskirts of Basle, past the main hospital and Spelentor because he said that it was something she could see, if only briefly.

The foyer was full when they reached the hotel; he bade her goodnight in the entrance, reminded her that they were to spend the morning together, and drove away. On her way to the lifts she encountered Sadie.

'You didn't come to dinner, honey.'

'No, I went out . . . '

'Fast worker, aren't you?' Sadie grinned. 'Anyone I know?'

Before she could reply she exclaimed, 'Hey, you're from London; so is that dream man who gave the lecture this evening. It's him!'

'Well, yes. You see, I'm his theatre sister, but it's not what you're thinking. I'm hoping to marry someone— he's something in television, and Professor van Teule is going to get married shortly. It's just pure chance that we happened to meet.'

Sadie considered this. 'Do you mean to say that you work for him and he never even hinted that he'd be here? He must have known that you'd be one of the crowd.'

'I dare say he forgot. We get on well, but only on a professional footing.' Which wasn't quite true. 'Don't spread it around, will you, Sadie?'

'Not me, honey. I'm no bigmouth. What's your man like?'

Rachel spent the next ten minutes describing Melville in loving detail.

The Professor called for her directly after breakfast the next morning. 'Strasbourg would be the obvious place but I don't think we can do it in the time we've got and in this car. We'll go to Kolmar. It will be packed with tourists but we'll take the road by the river and then cross over and come back on the other side.'

He started the car. 'It's the visit to the hospital this afternoon, isn't it? And my lecture this evening. Only an hour—there's a meeting I have to attend at eight o'clock. I should have liked to have taken you out for dinner but I can't get out of this particular gathering. Will you dine with me tomorrow and on Saturday?'

They were running beside the river and she stared at the splendid scenery. 'Thank you, I'd like to. We go home on Sunday—there's a midday flight.'

'Yes, I'm flying to Schiphol, having a couple of days at my home.'

To see the girl you are going to marry? wondered Rachel. Perhaps she is staying with his family. She wondered if she would phone Melville when she got back; after all, he must have wondered where she had got to. If he was free they might go out for the evening; she wasn't on duty until one o'clock the next day.

'A penny for them?' murmured the Professor.

It didn't enter her head to dissemble. 'I was wondering if I'd ring Melville when I get back.'

He shook his head. 'You'll never learn, Rachel.' His voice was gently mocking. 'But I should think that there will be a letter waiting for you, or at least a bouquet and a phone message.'

They parked the car in Kolmar, attractively mediaeval with vineyards all around it, had coffee and wandered round the market, looked inside the church and then crossed the river and drove back along the highway until the Professor turned off to go inland. 'There's time for a sandwich,' he told her. 'There's a place where we can get something to eat in Baden-weiler.'

It was a small inn in the tiny spa, hidden away in the Black Forest. They ate rolls and sausage and cheese and drank lager, and the landlord came and talked to them once he discovered the Professor spoke fluent German. He was a nice old man who smiled and nodded at her and then asked a question of the Professor.

'What's he saying?' she asked.

'He thinks you are a pretty girl,' said the Professor easily.

She didn't see him to speak to for the rest of that day. The visit to the hospital was interesting and there was a discussion afterwards. His own lecture in the evening tied up with what they had seen that afternoon and when he had finished there was another discussion. She went to bed early after another buffet supper.

There were three lectures the next day and she was a little tired by the evening. All the same it was pleasant to see the Professor waiting for her in the foyer. Sadie had come down in the lift with her and clutched her arm when she saw him. 'Honey, there's the boyfriend. Leap to it.'

'He's not . . . ' began Rachel, but couldn't finish in case he heard.

They went to the same restaurant as before and had the same table and the Professor made no effort to entertain her, only talked gently of this and that and made sure that she ate her dinner. He took her back soon after they had finished and said goodnight at the entrance. 'Tomorrow evening?' he suggested. 'Same place if you like it. You're going to the children's hospital tomorrow, aren't you?'

'Your lecture is first,' she reminded him. 'Your last one.'

The final day was well filled. There were last-minute get togethers, the Professor's lecture and the visit to the hospital and in the evening over dinner they talked about the week's events, but not too seriously.

'Everything has been arranged for you?' he asked as they sat over their coffee.

'Oh, yes. We have to hand in our vouchers and pay any bills tomorrow morning after breakfast and be ready to leave at midday.' She asked diffidently, 'You'll be gone by then?'

'No, my flight is in the afternoon. I had a chat with George this morning; they haven't been too busy, but he was kind enough to remind me that it's take-in next week.'

He said goodnight at the hotel and she said, 'Thank you for giving me such a nice time, Prof . . . Radmer. I'll see you next week, I expect.'

She was up early in the morning, but so was the Professor, sitting patiently in a corner of the foyer where he had a good view of the reception desk. He had no intention of letting Rachel see him, only a wish to make sure that she was safely on her way home.

He watched her join the small crowd around the reception desk. There were several of the girls who had attended the conference with her, but the people in front of them had just arrived. The Professor gave them a cursory glance and then stood up and started strolling across the foyer. The man even now stretching out a hand for his room key while his other arm encircled a blonde, very pretty girl was Melville. At any moment he would turn round and Rachel would see him.

CHAPTER EIGHT

RACHEL looked up from checking her modest bills, straight into Melville's face. For a few seconds her whole face lit up, her softly curving mouth half open, then she saw the consternation on his face; more than that, angry irritation and blue eyes, suddenly hard. He recovered quickly.

'So this is where you're hiding,' he observed. 'Have you been here long? I haven't had a chance to ring the hospital; I thought you were still there.'

Rachel hadn't spoken; her mouth was dry and she couldn't get the words out. In any case, she wasn't sure what words to utter. She dragged her eyes away from his face and looked at the girl, the same girl she had seen with him going up the steps of his London flat, ignoring her now, tugging at Melville's arm.

'Darling, hurry up. I simply must have a shower, and you've got the key.'

He patted her arm. 'OK, darling, we're on our way.' He glanced at Rachel and away again. 'Well, see you around, Rachel. It was fun while it lasted. No hard feelings, eh?' He added airily, 'We're here on location,' and winked. 'With a holiday on the side, of course.'

The girl gave his arm another tug and he gave her a careless kiss on her cheek. 'Darling, don't be in such a hurry. Haven't you heard of "Off with the old love and on with the new"? I can't remember who said that but I'm following his advice.'

They had gone. Rachel stood quite still, her face white, looking at nothing in particular. The queue around her had moved on but she hadn't noticed. She didn't notice the Professor either. He said quietly, 'Give me those,' and took the bills and voucher from her hand. 'Go and sit down and don't move until I come.'

She did as she had been told; she didn't take in what had happened and certainly was in no fit state to think for herself. Presently he was back again, sitting beside her, saying nothing, watching the colour creep back into her pale face. He lifted a finger to a page and a tray of coffee was set on a small table before them. There was a glass of brandy there, too; he told her to drink it in a no-nonsense voice, and she did that before drinking the coffee he poured. She hadn't spoken and neither had he but presently she whispered, 'I should like to scream.'

'I've a better idea. We will go to your room—you don't have to vacate it until midday—and you will lie down on your bed and take a nap. Then we will talk.'

'What about?' Her voice was fiercely bitter. 'Being jilted—how to make a fool of a girl in six easy lessons?' The brandy was taking effect. 'I'd like to run for miles and never speak to anyone again. And I've got to go back and everyone will ask . . . '

For answer he took her arm, whisked her into a lift, took her key from her bag and urged her gently into her room. 'Lie down,' he said. 'I'll stay for a while.'

'There's no time,' she said distractedly, and burst into tears.

He sat quietly while she cried and after a while, when the sobs had changed to heaving breaths and snuffles, he got up, mopped her face dry with a handkerchief and studied it.

She looked a fright, her nose was red and eyes pink and puffy and her hair had come loose from its plait, but somehow it didn't seem to matter that the Professor should see her like that. She said forlornly, 'I'd better wash my face. I'm sorry that I've made such a fuss.'

Two tears ran down her cheeks and she brushed them away with the back of her hand. 'I'll have to get ready. I have to go back to the hospital.

He put his sopping handkerchief back into a pocket. 'Not neccessarily. You're in no fit state to travel on your own and certainly not to go near an operating theatre. I'm going to ring Miss Marks. Will you leave things to me, Rachel?'

She nodded. 'But can I stay on here or could I go straight home—just for a day to—to get used to the idea?'

'I'll take you back with me.' He was matter-of-fact. 'My mother will be delighted to have you and in a couple of days you will be able to face up to things again.'

'But I don't know your mother. I can't possibly . . . Why should you . . . ?'

He sighed gently. 'Of course you don't know my mother, you haven't met. And you can, you know. And why should I? My dear Rachel, from motives of pure selfishness; I prefer you to scrub for me than anyone else.'

He got up and picked up the phone. 'Go and wash your face while I get things sorted out.'

When she got back from the bathroom he was phoning someone in his own language. He hung up presently and said, 'I told Miss Marks that you had picked up a mild virus and that I would be taking you to my home to get over it. I suggested two or three days off.'

Rachel was jolted out of her misery for a moment by the notion of Miss Marks agreeing to anything so unusual. 'Did she mind?'

He smiled faintly. 'I didn't ask her. She agreed with me that a virus infection in the hospital was to be avoided at all costs.

'But that's not true—I haven't got a virus.'

'No. I can lie most convincingly when I need to.' He smiled again. 'My mother will be delighted to welcome you.' He looked her up and down. 'That's better. Slap on some make-up and do your hair while I see if I can get a seat on my plane.'

There seemed nothing unusual in sitting down before the mirror and doing what she could to her face and brushing out her hair while he went on with his phoning, booking her a seat and then ringing the reception desk.

She was twisting her plait into a tidy knot by the time he had finished.

'Do you feel up to eating some lunch?—not here. If your luggage is ready you can check out and we'll go to my hotel, collect my case, hand over the car and eat a sandwich.'

Just for a moment she thought she would cry again. He was being so kind—arranging everything, giving her an impersonal sympathy and blessedly not offering good advice.

'Don't dare weep,' he warned her and swept her out of the room and into the lift. In the half-empty foyer he sat her down out of sight behind a mass of greenery, checked out for her and then led her to the car outside. She was trembling when she got in, frightened that she might come face to face with Melville again. The

Professor glanced at her shaking mouth and said, 'Now, now,' in a fatherly way, and started the car. By the time they had reached his hotel she had pulled herself together again. She drank the orange juice he ordered for her, said that yes, she would like chicken sandwiches, and, when they came, made a brave effort to eat them. They had coffee afterwards while the Professor, never a chatty man, kept up a steady flow of inconsequential talk. Rachel hardly heard a word of what he was saying, only the sound of his voice soothed her and stopped her from thinking.

Their flight was at five o'clock; they had a cup of tea about half past three, took a taxi to the airport and in due course boarded the plane.

It was seven o'clock when they emerged from Schiphol and almost at once a short stout man came up to them. The Professor shook his hand and drew Rachel forward to meet him. 'This is Bratte—he looks after the family.' He introduced her and added, 'He's brought a car to meet us.'

A Mercedes, drawn up to the kerb close by. Bratte and the porter saw to the luggage while the Professor ushered Rachel into the front seat and got in beside her. He said something to the other man as he climbed into the back of the car and they laughed together before he started the car and drove off.

Rachel sat silent, and the Professor, after one quick look at her sad profile, made no attempt to talk to her. She stared out at the countryside, not seeing it, but only Melville's face, hearing his voice: 'Off with the old love, on with the new.' What a fool she had been; a silly young woman who should have known better. Well, it had taught her a lesson; she wouldn't believe any man if ever one said that he loved her. She had a good job and she was expert at it; the Professor had said so. She would be a career girl and end up on the very topmost rung of the ladder. The thought made her shudder inwardly, but it was the answer.

'Close your eyes and go to sleep,' said the Professor softly without looking at her, and, although she hadn't intended to do so, she did.

When she woke up the day was fading. The country on either side of the road stretched away as far as she could see, wide green fields with here and there clumps of trees. Farmhouses, huge barns at their backs, were dotted around at intervals. Here and there were lights twinkling and there was a narrow canal running beside the road.

'We're north of Leeuwarden—the capital town—going towards the coast. We shall be about another ten minutes. Did you have a good nap?'

'Yes, thank you.' She heard the quiet content in his voice and the sudden nervousness she had felt melted away.

The road curved into a large clump of trees and then, unexpectedly, a village. Small, neat houses bordered the road leading to a cobbled square dominated by a jelly-mould church and surrounded by more houses— some of them quite large and most of them old.

Rachel, wide awake now, stared around her as the Professor circled the church slowly and took a narrow road on the further side.

The road was a brick one, tree-lined and with the canal still beside it. Presently there was a bridge with wrought iron gates at its further end opening into a cobbled drive.

The Professor had perforce to slow down which gave Rachel a chance to look around her. There were thick shrubberies on either side with trees beyond, so that she could see very little to the left or right, but as the drive curved she saw the house ahead of them. The evening was far advanced by now but she could see it clearly enough in the dusk for lights streamed from the windows. It was a square house, like a child's drawing, its windows set in rows on either side and above its massive front door, its roof set squarely upon it without gables or embellishment of any sort. Yet it had dignity and a kind of agelessness.

The Professor stopped the car and got out to open her door and as she got out in her turn she saw the symmetrical flowerbeds before the house, outlined with foot-high box hedges. She sniffed appreciatively; the air was fragrant with summer flowers. It was very quiet, although somewhere a dog was barking; for the first time since she had seen Melville that morning, she felt that she could cope.

The Professor took her arm and urged her up the steps to the door, held wide by Bratte who had gone ahead. 'Welcome to my home,' said the Professor. 'Come and meet my mother and father.'

They crossed a vast, marble-floored hall and opened double doors into an equally vast room with a lofty ceiling, tall wide windows draped in velvet and a polished wooden floor covered with a silk carpet. The furniture was exactly right: great bow-fronted display cabinets along the walls, a rent table between the windows, a Frisian wall clock above an *armoire,* its marquetry in the style of Berain, flanked by a pair of eighteenth-century armchairs covered in Beauvais tapestry. Nicely blended with these were comfortable chairs, small lamp tables and two well-upholstered sofas each side of the hooded fireplace. From one of these, two people arose: a tall, rather stout lady of late middle years, dressed with great good taste and her grey hair swept back in a severe bun, and an even taller man, some years older and, from the look of him, unmistakably the Professor's father. The lady surged forward, embraced her son and turned her attention to Rachel. 'My dear, welcome. Radmer has told us about you and your splendid work at the hospital and I am so glad to meet you.'

She had seemed formidable at first sight, but she wasn't at all; she had a kind face and twinkling eyes and Rachel liked her. She liked the Professor's father, too, a quiet man of few words who put her at her ease at once.

No one mentioned the reason for her being there. She was swept upstairs by a small stout woman answering to the name of Mieke, who puffed her way up the handsome staircase at the back of the hall and along a wide gallery to one of the doors lining it. Her case was already there. Mieke opened a door, showing her a bathroom, beamed at her and went away, leaving Rachel to make a lightning tour of her room. It was a splendid apartment with a bed of some dark wood she couldn't recognise and a matching tallboy and sofa table. The windows were hung with chintz which matched the bedspread and there was a thick cream carpet on the floor. The bathroom was as luxurious as the bedroom and she prowled round, admiring the soaps and bath lotions and pile of pastel-tinted towels before tidying her person. Her face bore signs of the day's events, for she was pale and her eyelids were still puffy, but she didn't allow herself to think about that; she owed it to the Professor to behave sensibly. He had been kind; how kind she was only just beginning to realise.

The Professor was waiting for her when she went downstairs. 'Hungry?' he wanted to know. 'I am. Mother and Father decided not to dine; they will have supper with us. Come and have a drink first.'

She was grateful to him for being so matter-of-fact; sympathy would undoubtedly have sent her off into floods of tears again. She drank the sherry she was offered and presently sat down in the dining-room, a little overawed by its magnificence. It was a large room, its crimson walls hung with numerous paintings. The oval mahogany table could seat sixteen persons in comfort and the chairs were ribbon-back Hepple-white. Along one wall was a vast serving table laden with silver and presided over by Bratte. It could have been rather overpowering but somehow it wasn't; Rachel did her best to eat the delicious food set before her and bore her share of the conversation, but it was relief when they had gone back to the drawing-room and, after a little more desultory talk over the coffee cups, her hostess suggested that she must be tired and longing for her bed. 'We breakfast early, at eight o'clock, my dear, but if you would prefer to have a tray in bed you have only to say so.'

Radmer got to his feet. 'Mother, dear, Rachel speaks no Dutch. She wouldn't know what to say. I'll knock on her door at half-past seven on my way down.'

'Oh, but I'll get up—there's no need . . . '

'All the same I shall knock.' He waited while she bade her host and hostess good night and walked with her to the door and opened it. 'Sleep well, Rachel,' he said quietly. His eyes searched her face. 'Would you like a sleeping pill?'

She shook her head. 'I'm tired. Beside, I have to think.'

He nodded. 'By all means do that, but remember that ideas and plans are always out of all proportion to the original in the early hours.'

He waited by the open door until she had gone upstairs and, she did her best to walk jauntily up the wide staircase, her back very straight.

She cried herself to sleep, of course. She had enough good sense to know that in time she would get over the hurt of it all, but Melville's words were still very clear in her head and she winced each time she remembered them; it wasn't very much good her telling herself that she would take good care never to fall in love again. The thought that Melville might discover that he had been wrong and loved her after all persisted in the back of her head; it was still there when she finally went to sleep.

A young girl with a round cheerful face brought her tea at seven o'clock, smiling broadly, pulled back the curtains and went away again. The smile had only widened at Rachel's good morning but she had waved an expressive arm at the bright morning outside before she went away.

Rachel nipped out of bed and took a look. Her room was at the back of the house, overlooking a large formal garden and what looked like a shrubbery beyond it. The windows opened on to a balcony. She lifted the sash and stepped outside, only to rush back in at a knock on the door.

'Morning,' said Radmer's voice from the other side of it. 'Coming down or breakfast in bed?'

'Oh, good morning. I'm coming down.'

He said, 'Good,' in a casual way and went, and she hurried to shower and dress, to go downstairs half an hour later in time to meet Radmer coming in through the front door, two Jack Russells at his heels. His, 'Hello,' was friendly, followed by, 'I hope you slept well?' uttered in an impersonal tone that needed no more than a brief reply. That she had been crying was obvious, but he offered no sympathy. He merely expressed the hope that she was hungry and opened the door to a small room behind the dining-room where breakfast had been set out on a round table at which his mother was already sitting. Her good morning was warm and friendly and her enquiry as to whether Rachel had slept well was as brief as her son's had been. 'Your father is down at the stables taking a look at the new foal. We won't wait for him.'

The meal was a pleasant one, unhurried and enlivened by Mevrouw van Teule's comments on every topic under the sun. She was, Rachel reflected, rather like her own mother, and, despite her somewhat intimidating appearance, just as motherly.

Breakfast over and still no sign of Mijnheer van Teule, she told them not to waste the morning. 'Lunch will be at twelve o'clock but it won't matter if you are late. We'll have it outside on the terrace.'

'Would you like a walk?' asked the Professor. 'There's a river beyond the shrubbery.'

'Well, if there is nothing you want to do . . . '

'Nothing. Let's go.'

They had crossed the formal garden and were deep into the shrubbery when he asked, 'Want to talk?'

He was strolling along, his hands in his pockets, not looking at her.

'What would be the use?' She tried hard not to sound sorry for herself. 'I've been a fool, haven't I? And now I'll just have to get over it. I don't suppose talking about it will help.'

'If it's any comfort to you, we've all been fools in our time. And of course talking will help. I expect you lay awake for hours wondering just what you would say to him if he were to turn up swearing eternal devotion.'

'He won't.' She was suddenly fierce. 'Not after the things he said. "Off with the old love"—if ever I was a love at all.' She stopped to stare up at the Professor. 'Doesn't it make any difference at all that I loved him?'

'Probably not.' His voice was cool. 'There are so many different kinds of love, Rachel. But you can always try again when you get back to London; I don't suppose they'll be on location for more than a week or so. Go and see him and don't, whatever you do, weep.' He smiled suddenly. 'Come and see the river.'

It was a small river, more a stream, running unhurriedly between green fields where the black and white cows stood about it in the sun.

They sat down on the grass and Rachel said, 'You must be very happy to come here after London and the hospital.'

'Oh, I am, but of course I enjoy my work and there are certain ties in London.'

His fiancée—she had forgotten her for the moment. 'Does she like it, too?' She glanced at his placid face. 'The girl you are going to marry?'

'Why, yes, she does. What are you going to tell your friends when you get back?'

'I won't need to say anything at first, will I? Only that he is out of the country. And—and by the time he is back I'll be able to talk about it without, without . . .'

'Bursting into tears. Delay the breaking of your heart, Rachel, until you have seen Melville. Chin up, stiff upper lip, squared shoulders; I have always thought of you as a young woman who could face up to things.'

She gave a shaky laugh. 'You sound like my eldest brother giving me sound advice.' She gave a watery sniff. 'Have you sisters, Radmer?'

'Four—all married. So you see I'm quite qualified to take your brother's place.' He said very deliberately, 'I'm a good deal older than you are, Rachel—thirty-five.'

'Oh, are you? I've never thought about it.'

His firm mouth twisted a little. 'You have had no reason to do so, have you?'

'No. Oh, Radmer, I don't know what to do. I always thought I was such a sensible person. What shall I do?'

He was lying back, his hands behind his head, his eyes half shut. 'I think I am the last person to tell you to do anything, Rachel. It is your life and you must decide how you want to live it.'

She felt her cheeks grow hot; it was the gentlest of snubs but it made her feel as though she was a silly girl trying to get sympathy. She said, 'Yes, of course,' and then, 'May we cross the river or is that someone else's land?'

He turned his head to look her, studying her profile, watching the colour ebb away. 'It's our land. There is a narrow ditch which is the boundary between us and the farm you can see over there. By all means let us walk on the other bank—there is another bridge at the far end of the field.'

Not another word was spoken about Melville, only as they strolled along he told her that he had phoned her mother. A remark which brought her up short, to raise a guilty face to his. 'I forgot—oh, how could I? Thank you for letting her know.' Her eyes looked a question she didn't want to ask.

'I told her that you were tired after your week and would be staying here for a day or so. You can ring her when you get back or from here if you wish.'

'I'll wait, I think. She knows I'm all right . . . Thank you, Radmer.'

She wanted to say more, to thank him more warmly, but he had offered her an inch of help and she had behaved as though it were an ell. She would take care not to talk about herself, not to really take advantage of his kindness. She asked too brightly, 'When are we going back?'

His voice was as placid as ever. 'Do you feel equal to taking a flight tomorrow evening? We don't need to leave until after tea and we can be at the hospital before midnight. But say if you'd rather wait a day or two. Are you on duty the following morning? Can you remember the off-duty rota?'

Of course she remembered it, although she didn't say so. After all, she had to worry over it every two weeks; by the time it was done to her satisfaction, she knew it off by heart. 'Yes, I'm on at eight o'clock—it should be your list.'

'I'll give George a ring presently. Shall we go back to the house? I dare say you'd like coffee or a drink of some sort.'

His mother and father were on the terrace and the dogs raced to meet them. Rachel sat down beside her hostess, drank her coffee and answered the string of questions, casually asked, which that lady embarked upon. She really was a dear, thought Rachel, explaining where her home was and agreeing that living in the country was so much nicer than in town. 'Though it makes a difference where you live,' she pointed out. 'It's very noisy at the hospital but it's not in the best part of London.'

'Radmer lives pleasantly enough,' observed his mother. 'The Bodkins look after him very well.'

'A good thing, too,' said Rachel warmly. 'He works frightfully hard, you know.'

'I am sure he does, my dear,' said his mother comfortably. 'It will be a good thing when he is married and has a wife.'

Rachel was surprised to discover that she didn't want to talk about that. I'm getting mean, she thought. Just because things haven't worked out for me, there is no reason why he shouldn't be happy. She resolutely shut her mind from her own unhappiness and asked Mevrouw van Teule to tell her the history of the house.

Radmar took her into Leeuwarden in the afternoon and accompanied her patiently round the Frisian Museum. He was very knowledgeable about his country; she listened with interest while he told her about Great Pier's enormous sword and the fourteenth-century drinking horn of the St Anthony Guild of Stavoren and explained the mediaeval costumes and paintings. They went from there to Franeker, so that she might see the planetarium and the beautiful Renaissance town hall before driving back to his house.

They had stopped for tea in one of the hotels and the conversation had been about Leeuwarden and Friesland. Even if she had wanted to, she had been given no opportunity to brood. Once back at his home, she had changed into another dress and joined everyone else for drinks before dinner and after that elegant and leisurely meal, they had sat outside on the terrace and she had found herself beside Radmer's father, who talked at some length about Friesland, shooting questions at her from time to time so that she had to pay attention. There had been simply no chance to think about herself all day, she reflected, tumbling into bed and going to sleep at once.

After breakfast the next morning Radmer stowed her into the car once more and drove north to the coast. The villages here were widespread, the cottages built on either side of dykes, and the roads were narrow and for the most part of brick. They had strange names, too; Radmer laughed at her attempts to pronounce them. Presently he said, 'Here's the sea.'

Zoutkamp, a shrimp-fishing centre where they stopped for coffee in a small dark cafe, where the coffee was excellent. They drove on, down a narrow country road skirting the Lauwers Meer until they joined the main road again, running close to the sea and then inland to Dokkum and so back to his home.

They were just in time for lunch and in the afternoon, despite her protestations that she must pack, he drove her across country to Oostermeer and then took the narrow brick roads to Grouw, where they had tea sitting by the water, watching the yachts spinning over the lake. They were back by four o'clock, to a second cup of tea, and then it was time for Rachel to pack her case once again.

They drove away with Bratte in the back so that he could take the car back and the warmth of her host's and hostess's goodbyes ringing in her ears. Two days had never gone so quickly and she had enjoyed every moment of them, she thought guiltily, but only because she had been given no chance to be by herself for one single minute—only at bedtime, and then she had been so pleasantly tired that she had slept at once.

Bratte saw them to the very exit gate, bidding the Professor goodbye and *Tot Ziens* and shaking her hand with the hope that he might see her again. They didn't have long to wait. They went aboard in the darkening evening, and, obedient to the Professor's suggestion, she refused the plastic tray of food and accepted the coffee she was offered. 'We'll eat at Heathrow,' he told her.

It still wanted two hours to midnight by the time they had retrieved their bags and gone through customs. Rachel was surprised to see the Professor's car outside the exit; travelling with him was certainly trouble free, she reflected, settling into the front seat.

But not for long. He drove to the Penta Hotel, parked the car and ushered her inside. 'Don't worry,' he said in answer to her look, 'I said you would be in the hospital by midnight and you will. Let's eat.'

She discovered that she was hungry. They ate steak and a salad and finished with a pot of coffee before they got into the car again and drove the sixteen miles to London. It was ten minutes to midnight when he drew in the hospital courtyard, opened her door, got her case, and walked to the entrance with her. The night porter was in his box, reading the paper; he glanced up and then back to the page. The Professor pushed open the door and they went in. He walked with Rachel across the hall to the door leading to the nurses' home, opened it, put the case inside and said, 'I don't dare to go a step further and certainly not at this hour of night. You are all right, Rachel?'

She lifted a grateful face to his. 'Yes, thank you very much—I can't thank you enough, Radmer—and I must stop calling you that now, mustn't I? I'll see you in the morning.'

She smiled at him, making a brave attempt to behave normally.

'Goodnight, Rachel.' He bent his head suddenly and kissed her hard on her surprised mouth, turned on his heel and walked away.

She picked up her case and started up the stairs. She had been feeling dreadful, rejected, undesirable, not worth a second look, but somehow his kiss had changed that. Somewhere, right at the bottom of her unhappiness, there was a small spark; she wasn't sure what it was, only that her cold insides were warmed by it.

None of her friends were still up. She crept to her room, had a bath, unpacked and got into bed, thankful that there would be a great deal to occupy her in the morning. A wave of misery swept over her, swamped almost at once by sleep.

As is always the case, the misery was easier to bear in the morning. Rachel went down to breakfast, answered the questions with which she was bombarded and hurried along to the theatre wing. Norah was already there, delighted to have her back; the moment the night sister had gone, she produced a fistful of requests and notes for Rachel to deal with. The CSD were cutting up rough again, the laundry had rung to say that they were using too many sheets and towels, two nurses wanted days off for something special and Mrs Pepys had rung to say that she had a migraine and wouldn't be in for her normal duty.

'Did anything nice happen?' asked Rachel and they laughed together.

The theatre list was on her desk. A heavy one, but then it always was when the Professor was operating. Rachel organised the day's work, rang down to Woman's Surgical to make sure that the first patient was ready and went along to theatre.

Sidney was brooding over his equipment and was obviously glad to see her. So were the nurses. She checked everything was ready for the first case and went to scrub. She could hear the whine of the lift bringing the patient to theatre and turned her head to wish Dr Carr good morning as he poked his head round the door to see if she was there.

'Better?' he wanted to know, and she remembered just in time that she had had a virus, and said that yes, she was fine again. When the list was finished she would have to go the office and see Miss Marks.

She was being tied into her gown when the Professor came in to scrub. His 'Good Morning, Sister' was uttered with a detached friendliness and he turned away at once to speak to George. She wasn't sure what she had expected but certainly not this polite indifference. She went into the theatre and checked her trolleys and cast an eye around before checking with Norah who should be sent to coffee first and which of the nurses should go into the sluice.

The Professor, with George and Billy, was standing away from the table while the patient was arranged just so and Dr Carr checked the anaesthetics, and Rachel, with nothing to do for the moment, allowed her thoughts to dwell on him. He was quite right, of course. He had helped her when she had needed help, but the circumstances had been unusual and now they were back, leading their normal lives once more. At least he was; she still felt as though she were in a bad dream and at the moment all she longed for was to recapture the quiet orderly life she had led before she had met Melville.

The patient was deeply unconscious. Dr Carr said 'She's ready when you are, Radmer,' and sat back on his stool, all his attention on the quiet face before him, the signal for Rachel to hand towels and clips and then scalpel and forceps, her well-trained mind concentrating on her work.

The list lasted several hours, and when they paused for coffee half-way through the talk was about the cases. No one mentioned Basle at all and Rachel supposed that they had already discussed it before they got to theatre. Only at the end of the list when the men had gone to the changing room and she was organising the clearing up did Billy poke his head round the door to ask, 'Did you have a good time, Rachel? You don't look quite your usual smashing self. Did they work you too hard?'

She hadn't bothered to take off her mask, only pulled it under her chin, and she still wore her theatre cap, but that didn't detract from her pretty face. She gave him a grin. 'Not a bit of it; just lectures and things, you know, but there were rather a lot of them.'

'It must have been great. Pity about the virus.'

The Professor had lounged into theatre, on the point of leaving. 'Nasty things, virus infections. Billy, I want you to go to Men's Surgical and check on Mr Willis—he's for the end of the week, isn't he? He's been running a temperature.' He looked across at Rachel. 'Sister, I've a kidney transplant lined up as soon as it's possible to do it. Can you get your extra staff at short notice?'

'Yes, sir.' She was pleased with her coolly efficient voice. 'I'll warn the part-timers and the nurses here.'

'Good, thank you.' He nodded with the faintest of smiles and went away. Watching his broad back so impeccably clothed, she found it hard to equate his elegant image with the casually dressed friend who had listened so patiently to her as they sat by the little stream at his home.

She pushed her cap further back on her head and began to bundle the instruments, ready to be collected by the CSD. Best not to waste time thinking; next week she would go home on her days off and sort herself out in the peace and quiet of the country.

CHAPTER NINE

DESPITE the fact that her days were fully occupied, Rachel found that they dragged. It seemed as if her days off would never come, but at last they did. She flung things into her overnight bag, got into the Fiat and drove herself home. She had hardly spoken to the Professor since they had returned. Beyond enquiring as to whether Miss Marks had accepted her excuse of a virus infection without fuss, he had had very little to say to her except for their normal exchanges regarding theatre lists and the like. It was as though he were standing at a distance, watching her; a silly fantasy she instantly dismissed. She had been sleeping badly, too, waking in the night to remember far too clearly Melville's cruel remarks about being off with the old love. During the day she resolutely put him out of her mind, but at night it was a different matter; at home, perhaps she would sleep soundly.

She had phoned her mother when she got back to England with the Professor but she had said nothing about Melville; that could wait until she and her mother were alone some time during her brief stay at home. As she drove she thought about the Professor, wondering if she had annoyed him in some way, but discarding the idea. It seemed more likely that he regarded her as a possible embarrassment, seeing that he was thinking about getting married; perhaps he was expecting her to take advantage of his kindness while she had been in Basle. 'Well, he's quite wrong,' said

Rachel loudly, and then, 'All the same, I wish I knew what was the matter . . . '

She had left the hospital in the early evening but the traffic was heavy and it was late when she got home at last. Her parents were waiting for her, and over her supper she gave them an expurgated account of her week in Basle, aware that it was only too obvious that she was leaving out a great deal. But her mother and father said nothing to that effect, merely observing that it had been an experience, and that it must have been a tiring week for her. 'Though your brothers are green with envy,' said her mother. 'Edward and Nick are going to Scotland during the holidays camping but they are already talking about hitchhiking round Europe.'

Her room welcomed her: all her childhood furniture, her dolls sitting in a row on the shelf her father had made for them, flowers in a bowl on the dressing-table. She unpacked her few things and went to bed and slept all night, although she hadn't expected to.

She told her mother everything the next morning while they were sitting in the garden, shelling peas. It was easier than she had expected, partly because she had something to do while she talked. Her mother didn't interrupt; now and again she made soothing murmurs and once drew in her breath sharply when Rachel repeated what Melville had said at the hotel. Rachel had finished and was blowing her nose in an effort not to cry when she spoke. 'I'm sorry you're unhappy, love, but look at it this way, you would have been even more unhappy if you had gone on seeing Melville, expecting to marry him, no doubt. Infatuation makes one blind but the nice part is that sooner or later you see again and it becomes something that doesn't matter at all.' She glanced sideways at her daughter's unhappy face. 'Professor van Teule was very kind—I wrote a letter to his mother, just to thank her, and she wrote back saying how much they had enjoyed having you. I suppose he's back at the hospital too?' The question was put so casually that Rachel answered without hesitation.

'Oh, yes. He had a list the morning after we got back.'

'So you've had a chance to talk about the conference . . . '

Rachel frowned. 'Plenty, but we haven't. You see, Mother, it's all over and done with now, I expect he wants to forget it. He told me weeks ago that he hoped to get married soon.'

Her mother shelled quite a few peas before she said, 'I wonder what she's like . . . '

'I've no idea. He never talks about himself and no one mentioned her when I was at his home. He did say that she liked his father's house.'

'Ah well, I dare say you'll meet her one day.' There was regret in her mother's voice but Rachel didn't notice it.

'I don't expect so. Actually, we've hardly spoken since we came back.' She sighed soundlessly. 'We've always been on good terms but we aren't any more. He's—he's gone all distant.'

'What a pity,' observed Mrs Downing, and meant it.

Rachel went back on the following evening considerably refreshed. She had walked miles with Mutt, called on friends in the village, driven her father on his afternoon rounds and helped around the house, and she felt content. She refused to think about Melville but she had to admit to herself that she was glad that she wouldn't have to meet any of his friends again. All those clothes in my cupboard, she reflected, and chuckled for the first time in days. And no more agonising over her face and hair either. She remembered then how she had sat at her dressing-table, putting herself to rights while the Professor had sat beside her, telephoning. She hadn't given it a thought then because for some reason she hadn't minded him seeing her looking a mess. She frowned a little over that; perhaps she had been in a state of shock. On the other hand she had to admit that if the same circumstances should arise again, she would think nothing of it. 'Very odd,' she said out loud.

It began to rain as she neared the hospital. It was an ugly building at the best of times; now it looked downright hideous and she would have to live and work in it, probably for years, until or unless she went somewhere else. She would get a post easily enough, she was a good theatre sister and the world was her oyster, but somewhere at the back of her mind was a niggling reluctance to leave the place.

She parked the Fiat and went through to her room, pausing, because she hadn't been able to stop herself, by the letter racks to see if there were any letters for her. There was one envelope, from the Professor, containing a brief note; he hoped that she wouldn't be greatly inconvenienced if he started his list half an hour earlier than usual—abdominal injuries—a man too shocked for immediate operation. It was signed with his initials.

Businesslike in the extreme, she thought, but only to be expected. She turned round and made her way up to the theatre wing and sat down at her desk in the office and checked the off duty book. There would be enough nurses on duty during the morning. She would have her breakfast early so that she could check theatre

before she started to scrub. The night staff nurse was
on duty; Rachel asked her to get things started ready
for the morning's work and then went along to her
room, her personal difficulties ousted for the moment
by plans for the morning.

The morning went well, just as hundreds of others
had. The Professor was his usual calm self, George and
Billy cheerfully friendly, the nurses on their mettle. The
list was finished by half past one and Rachel went down
to the canteen to consume cottage pie and cabbage,
stewed prunes and custard. This uninspired menu set
her in mind of the previous week's food, way ahead of
what was on her plate at the moment. She didn't allow
her thoughts to dwell on it but dranktwo cups of very
strong tea and then went back totheatre.

The next day or so were uneventful but fortunately
for her very busy. She had little time to brood and, to
her relief, none of her friends had mentioned Melville
once. If she had thought about this she might have
found it strange, but she was almost feverish in her
endeavour not to think of him at all.

The week had almost gone by when she was warned
at the end of the day's work that there was a real possi-
bility of a kidney transplant within the next few hours.
She set about getting organised, warning in her turn
the nurses she would need, seeing that the second
theatre was ready for use for any emergency, phoning
the faithful Sidney. She scrubbed and laid up in read-
iness and then went to the sisters' sitting-room to await
events.

She had had supper and had gone back to sit curled
up in a chair, reading the day's news, before George
phoned and told her that they would operate in an
hour's time. She put her cap on, slipped her feet back
into her shoes and went back to theatre. The night staff

nurse, whom she had warned, was already there and there was almost nothing to do. Rachel warned Sidney, made sure that the path lab, X-Ray department and the dispensary had been told, told the staff nurse to make tea and checked the theatre once more.

Half an hour later she gathered her nurses around her, replaced her cap with a theatre mob cap and went to scrub. If all was going well Dr Carr would be along with his patient within the next ten minutes. Everything was just as it should be as the Professor walked in. He made no apology for there was no need; everyone there knew that transplants took place to no set timetable. The operation started and no one so much as glanced at the clock.

The patient was a teenage boy with little chance of a normal life without a transplant; everyone in the theatre would willingly have spent twice as long there if it had been necessary. It wasn't; the Professor completed his work, pronounced himself satisfied and the patient was borne away to the recovery room and then to the intensive care unit. The Professor thanked his companions, and wandered out of the theatre with George in close attendance, Rachel, already busy with the clearing up, nodded to one of the nurses to go and get the coffee from the kitchen. The men would need a drink; she could do with one herself. When the worst of the clearing away had been done, she sent the nurses off duty, and began on the wearying task of readying the theatre for the morning, now only four or five hours away.

It was another half-hour before she was ready to leave. The night runner was in the sluice; Rachel wished her goodnight and went along to her office.

The Professor was there, standing by the window, looking out into the night. He glanced over his shoulder as she went in. 'Finished?' he asked.

'Very nearly, sir.' She sat down at the desk and began to record the operation in her neat handwriting, suddenly conscious of her capless head and shining nose, made all the worse by the elegance of the Professor's appearance.

She closed the book and he said quietly, 'Go to bed, Rachel.'

She stood up. 'You wanted something, Professor?'

He strolled to the door. 'Oh, yes, but not just at the moment.' He paused at the door and turned to look at her. His smile was amused and tender and her eyes widened. Melville had never looked at her like that and she didn't know what to make of it, and she had no way of finding out because he had gone with a quiet, 'Goodnight.'

She told herself as she tumbled into bed that she had imagined his look; she was tired and still feeling the sharpness of her break with Melville. She was too sleepy to admit that she didn't feel anything of the sort.

She didn't see the Professor the next day and for some reason she felt peevish, ticking off the nurses with unwonted sharpness and even biting Norah's head off over some trivial matter. She apologised immediately, adding in a bewildered manner, 'I don't know what's the matter with me, Norah. At least I don't think so.' She hadn't told anyone about Melville, not even Lucy, but now suddenly it didn't matter any more if everyone knew. 'I saw Melville in Basle—with another girl. He told me plainly that we were finished. It was a blow but I think my pride was more hurt than my heart. It—it was a bit of a surprise.'

'No one ever thought he was good enough for you,' declared Norah stoutly. 'He'll make a rotten husband—if he ever marries.'

'So why do I feel so wretched?'

Norah preserved a prudent silence, only murmuring nothings. She had her own ideas about that.

Rachel discovered the answer for herself the next morning. She had been to the dispensary to do battle with the dispenser, a middle-aged acidulated man who dispensed his pills and medicines as though they were drops of his life blood. Rachel had spent five minutes of valuable time upon prising a bottle of surgical spirit from the miserly grasp and now, flushed with triumph, started on her way back to the theatre wing. There were several routes she could take; she chose the one which would take her past the letter racks. Tom had told her that he and Natalie were intending to marry quite soon and as soon as they had decided on a date, he would let her know. There might be a letter from him. There was. Tucking it into her pocket, she turned round too find the Professor right behind her.

'Melville?' he asked.

'Melville.' She repeated the name as though she had never heard it before. 'No—my brother Tom, he's going to be married. He said he'd write and tell me the date.'

The Professor's face remained impassive at this news, although his eyes gleamed beneath their lids. He said nothing, just stood there looking at her and she stared back, going slowly pink in the face. Her mother had been quite right; she had said that sooner or later she would see again, and she saw now with a clarity which took her breath away and sent her heart racing. Melville might never have been; it was this gentle giant she loved, and why hadn't she realised it before? She had always been at ease with him, she had howled her eyes out in front of him and not felt in the least ashamed of it, she had even sat down and done her hair and face without giving his presence a thought. Oh, she had been as blind as a bat and now, too late, she wasn't. A pity she hadn't stayed blind, then she wouldn't have minded in the least that he was going to marry. The appalling thought struck her that he knew exactly what she was thinking.

She said in a high voice not in the least like her usual serene tones, 'I have to get back to theatre . . . Surgical spirit,' she added inanely, and, because he was smiling now, 'The instrument cupboards,' she babbled and whisked past him, cheeks still hot, chaotic thoughts tumbling around in her head, to get away as far as possible and never see Radmer again. The thought was so agonising that she dismissed it at once. Indeed, if her heart had had its way she would have turned round and run straight back and flung herself into his arms. Which, of course, wouldn't do at all. Common sense took over: she went into theatre, dealt with a difference of opinion between Mrs Pepys and the senior student nurse, threatening to reach alarming proportions, checked that the second theatre was ready for Mr Sims, who had a short list that morning, and went to her office. Norah would scrub for Mr Sims and when he'd finished Mrs Pepys could take the dental list. It was a quiet day workwise; she would get the off-duty rota seen to, catch up on the various forms she was required to fill in from time to time and go off duty at five o'clock, wash her hair and have an early night.

She had been sitting at her desk doing nothing at all for all of ten minutes when the phone rang. It was Miss Marks and at the sound of her voice Rachel hastily reviewed the last few days, trying to remember if anything had gone wrong. Mrs Pepys was always threatening to go to the office about this, that and the other; she supposed it was something to do with her.

'Sister Downing,' Miss Marks's voice sounded severe. 'Will you go to the consultants' room now. Professor van Teule wishes to speak to you.'

'Whatever for?' asked Rachel, forgetting all about being civil to one's superiors at all times.

'I do not know, Sister,' Miss Marks's voice was rebuking. 'I presume he will tell you. Be good enough not to keep him waiting.' She rang off and Rachel got up and went to peer in the mirror to see if her cap was on straight and her nose wasn't shining. At the moment she could think of no reason why the Professor should want to see her and she was to be given no time in which to speculate about it. She went to tell Norah and then made her way to the wide corridor on the other side of the entrance hall where the consultants spent any spare time they had in comfort.

She tapped on the door and went in and the Professor, sitting on the edge of the massive table in the centre of the room, got up and came towards her. She did her best to be her usual calm self; she had become a little pale at the thought of seeing him and her eyes were full of questions, but she had clenched her hands to stop their trembling and when she spoke her voice was almost normal.

'You wanted me, sir?'

He had come to a halt before her. 'I've wanted you for a long time now, Rachel.' He smiled a little at her look of utter surprise. 'But you didn't know that until an hour or two ago, did you?'

He paused and looked at her and she knew that he expected an answer. 'No, I didn't. Mother said . . . she said that infatuation had made me blind but that one day I'd see again.' She added very worriedly, 'But I don't think we ought to talk like this—you're going to marry, aren't you? I'm not sure what you wanted to see me about, but could we stop now? We've always been good friends and it would be nice to go on being that.

He said with a good deal of warmth, 'It would not be nice, it would be an untenable situation. I am in love with you, Rachel.'

She closed her eyes for a moment. The sheer joy of hearing him say that made her feel quite giddy, but only for a moment. She opened them again and looked at him steadily. 'I love you, too. I wouldn't have told you of course . . . ' She said loudly, 'Oh, this is a strange conversation in a most unsuitable pace. If Miss Marks knew she would have a stroke.'

'Let us forget Miss Marks. You said you loved me, it sounded nice. Will you say it again, my darling?'

'I'm not your darling. Oh, how can I be? Perhaps you're infatuated with me, like I was with Melville, and you'll wake up and look at your fiancée and know that you love her more than anything in the world.'

'I said you were my darling, and you are and you always will be. Listen to me now. Weeks ago I told you that I hoped to get married. From the simple statement you have fashioned a fiancée who doesn't exist. You silly girl, did it never enter your head that I might be in love with you?' He made 'silly girl' sound like an endearment.

'No, never.' She went close to him and put out a shy hand on to his sleeve. 'I thought of you as a friend. I didn't mind you seeing me when I cried or my hair fell down or I was tired, but I know now that it was all part of loving you, if you see what I mean. But you never . . . That is, I never thought that you loved me. Is that why you wanted to see me?'

His arms were round her, holding her very close. 'Yes, my dearest darling, it was.' He bent and kissed her and then kissed her again. 'Will you marry me, Rachel?'

'Oh, yes, of course I will!' Her pale face was beautifully pink now, and her eyes shone. 'When?'

He threw back his head and let out a bellow of laughter. 'If I had my way, this very minute, but there is the question of the licence. How about a week's time? Can we assemble the families by then, the church, the parson . . .'

'My dress.' She smiled up at him. 'If we really want to, we can.'

'We'll make it five days.' He kissed her slowly. 'Now we'll go and see Miss Marks.' And, at her look of enquiry, 'So that you can leave, dear heart.'

'She'll never agree . . .'

'I have a certain amount of influence,' said the professor with faint smugness. 'And we will invite her to be godmother to our firstborn.'

'She'll have to come to the wedding . . .'

'As far as I'm concerned, sweetheart, the entire world may come, just as long as you are there.'

She threw her arms around his neck. 'I'll always be there, I'll never want to be anywhere else.' A remark which gave the Professor so much satisfaction that he kissed her again, very thoroughly.

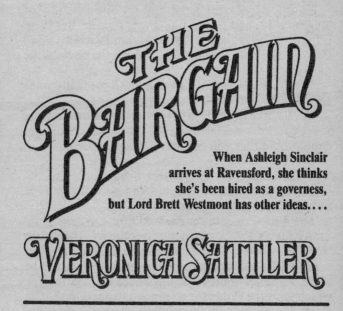

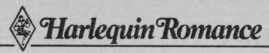
Harlequin Romance

Coming Next Month

2875 THE WAITING HEART Jeanne Allan
City schoolteacher Susan's Christmas holiday at the Colorado
ranch of her elderly friend Elizabeth is spoiled by Elizabeth's
son—a man who dominates everything and everyone. Expecting
to dominate Susan, too, he's surprised by her equally
strong resistance!

2876 THE HEART OF THE MATTER Lindsay Armstrong
All her young life Clarry has turned to Robert for help, so it seems
entirely natural when he saves her family home by marrying her.
Only now there is a price to pay—Clarry has to grow up....

2877 HEARTLAND Bethany Campbell
Budding cartoonist Toby is glad to help temporarily injured top
cartoonist Jake Ulrick—but it isn't easy. Cold, abrupt, a tyrant to
work for, he resents needing anyone. So it doesn't help matters
at all when Toby falls in love with him.

2878 AN ENGAGEMENT IS ANNOUNCED Claudia Jameson
Physiotherapist Anthea Norman cuts short her Canary Islands visit
when her hostess's attractive lawyer nephew zooms in for serious
pursuit. Instinct tells her to run. She doesn't want to experience the
heartbreak of loving and losing again....

2879 SELL ME A DREAM Leigh Michaels
Stephanie has built a career for herself in real estate as well as made
a home for her small daughter—the daughter Jordan doesn't know
about. And she's practically engaged to staid dependable Tony.
Now isn't the time for Jordan to come bouncing back into her life.

2880 NO SAD SONG Alison York
To achieve success in her operatic career, Annabel has to work with
Piers Bellingham, the top entrepreneur—and a man she detests. As
it turns out, working with Piers is not the problem. It's strictly
one of the heart!

Available in December wherever paperback books are sold,
or through Harlequin Reader Service.

In the U.S.
901 Fuhrmann Blvd.
P.O. Box 1397
Buffalo, N.Y. 14240-1397

In Canada
P.O. Box 603
Fort Erie, Ontario
L2A 5X3